The Rich Die Too

A Lee Cameron Mystery

by

Lowell Bergeron

Author's Note

I am dedicating this to those who like to read mysteries.

My other books available on Amazon

The New Kid
The Last Inning
Spirit of Jenny
Charlestown (A Civil War Novel)
Odds and Ends (Old Stories)
Early Flight Home (A Poetic Collection)

1

Thursday, November 18th

I like to look out windows. The view isn't important. It could be a scene across the city, a clump of trees, or a building next door. That's why I took the second-floor office in the Shelberg Bank Building. It has huge ceiling to floor windows facing the street. It gets hot as Hell in the summer, but the windows have the opposite effect during the cooler months. It's a balancing act for Mother Nature.

The weather was in the mid-sixties with a little mist in the air. The early Christmas shoppers scurried about. I thought it was a little early, only one week before Thanksgiving. Retailers drew out the shoppers earlier every year. I imagine it wouldn't be long before we start skipping all the holidays and go straight to Christmas at the beginning of the year.

One woman with a child, who looked old enough to be in school, trudged along with an armload of packages held in one hand. The little tyke screamed and resisted, trying to pull away from her other hand. She leaned forward. He leaned back. They looked like two tug-of-war teams fighting for that extra inch. I watched them until they were out of sight. I could see the mom winning the battle because they were moving in her direction, but it didn't stop the child from putting up the good fight.

My eyes wandered back to the crowd. They settled on a young man, who also looked old enough to be in school, but this kid looked to be in his mid-teens. He leaned against a nail shop across from the bank, one foot on the wall. His baseball cap was turned backwards so as not to interfere with his view. I could tell he was scoping out his next victim and paid close attention to the elderly women. He was your typical purse snatcher preying on those who can't defend themselves.

I clenched and unclenched my fists. I wanted to go down there and beat his head against the wall, but of course I didn't have a motive. He could be just hanging around meaning no one any harm, but I felt my suspicion would play out.

Sheila liked the holiday season. No, let me correct that. She loved the holiday season. She started as close to Thanksgiving as the law allowed and put up a little tree in her outside office. It looked like Santa's workshop. She hung mistletoe everywhere, put up a train set to choo choo around her tree, hung wreaths and holly to rival the mistletoe. She went to yard sales and bought old ornaments that she called "cute" and "sentimental." It is her favorite time of year, and she goes all out to celebrate it.

"Sentimental for who?" I asked her.

"For someone. Me, now."

The place was an obstacle course with things hanging from the ceiling and rolling around on the floor. Everything was green and red. I really had to be careful not to smash or kick something over.

She wanted to put a tree up in my office, but I said, "No thanks."

"Scrooge," was what came out, but I think she wanted to call me other things.

My name is Lee Cameron. That little piece of paper on my office wall claims my occupation to be a private detective. When you think about it, what was private about it? When you're sticking your nose into other people's business, it's hardly private and sometimes said nose gets smacked.

I'm not one of those television detectives who go around chasing bad guys for miles on end or getting into a twenty-mile car chase or bedding the women. It looks good in the movies, but it doesn't happen to me. Sheila would frown on it if I did, and she found out. I do deal with the part about chasing bad guys at times, but I'm glad it doesn't happen often.

On a personal note, I'm six feet tall and weigh in around 200. My wardrobe consists mostly of tee shirts (I like the ones with something on them, not plain), black jeans, and sneakers, what my parents' generation used to call tennis shoes. My hair is short and brown; my eyes are gray; my nose takes a slight turn to the right as a result of a battle with a baseball bat that said nose lost. All in all,

I'm an average guy who's average looking. That, of course, depends on who you talk to.

The morning edition of the Shelberg Beacon lay on my desk. There was some excitement last night, but no one knew about it until this morning. It screamed out a big headline:

LOCAL BUSINESSMAN FOUND DEAD
Foul play suspected

The businessman referenced was Edwin Barnett. His family is the richest in Louisiana and one of the wealthiest in the country.

While watching the people below, I wondered who would want to kill Mr. Barnett. Being money hungry as he was, there was always the possibility he stepped on some toes to get to where he was. Maybe the owner of one of those toes had enough and retaliated. This would be a tough case for Shelberg's finest: high profile with a lot of publicity. It would probably end up one of those cases where the nation wants to gobble up whatever it could about the wealthy dead.

I went to the little frig I keep in my office and took out my breakfast of choice, Diet Dr. Pepper in a bottle. My doctor wants me off sugar, so this is my second-choice drink next to the original stuff. I went to my desk and took a long drink then made sure I put the bottle on a coaster. Sheila furnishes them and expects everyone to use them. Rings on the furniture are one of her pet peeves and makes her very unhappy.

I picked up the paper and looked at the picture of Edwin Barnett from one of his better days. He was a good-looking guy who I'm sure could get his share of the ladies if he so desired. Money and looks go a long way, especially the money.

There was a knock on the door that separated the two offices and it opened before I could answer.

"You know, Sheila," I said without looking up from the paper. "One day you'll walk in here and catch me doing something you wouldn't want to see."

"You wish," she said coming up to my desk.

Sheila Arceneaux is my secretary. She's got shoulder length red hair complemented by bright blue eyes. She's a shade shorter than me. Her marriage ended in a messy divorce, but she never talks about it. I figure if she wants to tell me, she will in good time and I never ask about those scars on her forearms, but I often wonder what happened.

She sat down across from me.

"Edwin Barnett's murder is all over the radio."

I tapped the paper. "It says here he was found dead. He may have died of natural causes."

She leaned forward to see the front page then sat back. "It also says foul play is suspected. Does that sound like natural causes?"

"You in on the investigation?"

"You know I'm not, but I think you'll figure out some way to finagle your way in."

"Finagle? Is that your word for the day?"

"Finagle," she said, "according to Webster it means, the one that fits you is, to obtain by indirect or involved means. There are a couple more, but that is the nicest meaning referring to you."

"Wonderful, a walking dictionary. Just what I need."

She just smiled and what a beautiful smile it was.

I leaned back, looked at the ceiling, and spread my arms.

"What with all this business? When will I find the time?"

"We don't have one thing going right now and you know you're itching to know what's going on."

"I know no such thing."

I held my thumb and index finger about half an inch apart. "Well, maybe a little."

"Who do you think did it?"

I put my elbows on the desk and made a tepee with my hands, tapping my index fingers together.

"Why do you want to think someone killed him?"

"That man had too much money to die of natural causes."

"What does being rich have to do with dying of natural causes?"

"Never mind," she said sitting back and crossing those beautiful legs.

"He was in his early sixties. It's not old, but he was no spring chicken."

She waved her hand.

"Don't tell me you haven't been sitting here thinking about it. Come on, give."

"I would say someone who wasn't entirely happy with Mr. Barnett did him in. Of course, we could be way off base here. It could have been someone who was deeply in love with him."

"Ha ha. When one person kills another person, it is a given that the first person was not happy with the second person."

I cocked my head at her.

"Can you repeat that?"

"Never mind."

"Come," I said leading her to the window, "What do you see?"

By now the crowd had increased. The vehicle traffic was bumper-to-bumper with workers and shoppers jockeying for a place to park.

"Early Christmas shoppers," she said.

"Anything else?"

"Such as…"

"Any one of those people could have murdered Edwin Barnett."

"Oh, yeah? How about explaining your deduction?"

"The Barnett family partially or wholly owns a number of large banks and hotels. Since their companies are not public, I'll assume they also have other investments. Some could be apartment complexes, department stores, anything that customers patronize."

I pointed down to the street.

"It may be safe to say that some or all of the good people you see before us do business with one of more of the Barnett owned businesses. It could be someone who was mistreated at one of their establishments or felt they were cheated. It could be the customer or spouse, or both didn't take too kindly of the situation and decided it was time to change the head of the company. Maybe he bruised the ego of a politician or competitor. Anyone can commit murder given the right, or wrong, circumstances.”

I held an index finger up to her for emphasis.

“And let us not forget Edwin Barnett has, or had, a very attractive young wife. There’s that to consider. The possibilities are endless.”

“That was a nice little speech. Do you think his wife did it?”

“Only time will tell. One never knows.”

“No, one doesn’t,” she smiled.

“Look at that,” I said pointing to the teenage boy leaning against the nail shop across the street, “He’s looking for a victim.”

“Maybe he killed Edwin Barnett.”

I ignored her remark.

“I was watching him earlier,” I said.

A grandmotherly woman worked her way down the sidewalk with the aid of a cane. She carried a purse on her inside shoulder. The young man nodded to her. She nodded back. Then with a swift motion he grabbed at the purse. Grandma’s reflexes were faster than his. She brought the cane around in a wide speedy arc and crashed it against his head. The young wanna be robber dropped like a rock. The woman adjusted the purse on her shoulder and continued on her way. The crowd applauded her. She smiled and moved on.

“I could use her as a bodyguard,” I said.

“Maybe she killed Edwin Barnett.”

“She could have done a better job than her attacker. Why isn’t that kid in school, anyway?”

“Maybe the detention center let him off for good behavior,” Sheila said. “For the holidays.”

A man in a suit holding a briefcase stood over the boy and talked into his cell phone. A police cruiser showed up. The two officers spoke with the man while looking down the street. Finding nothing or no one they hauled the kid off. Grandma was long gone.

“I’ll bet that wasn’t the first time she’s been mugged,” Sheila said, “She carried that purse like she was baiting him.”

“We need more grandmothers like her.”

We returned to my desk. Sheila picked up the newspaper, sat down, and started to read.

"Local businessman and philanthropist, Edwin Barnett, was found dead in his office yesterday morning by his long-time secretary, Doreen Tilly. She dialed 911 after finding him slumped over his desk.

"Shelberg Police Detective Oliver Fletcher is leading the investigation. When questioned by this reporter, Mr. Fletcher stated it is still early in the investigation, but Mr. Barnett's death is being treated as a homicide. There is every indication, he said, of foul play. Natural causes my ass."

"Did the detective say that last line?"

"No, but you said natural causes. Now, where was I? Mr. Barnett's wife, Neda, was out of the country at the time. She was notified of her husband's passing by Miss Tilly. No one knows when she will return home. Yvonne Barnett, Mr. Barnett's mother, was understandably unavailable for comment. The rest is personal stuff. No mention of a funeral."

Then she scrunched up her face.

"And the article is written by that bitch, Crystal Hudson."

"Does it say article written by that bitch, Crystal Hudson?"

"No, it's my opinion."

"You know her."

"In passing."

"Did you pass some blows?"

She smiled. She smiles a lot when she doesn't want to answer my questions.

"Anyway," I said, "They'll do an autopsy first. When they release the body to the family, we'll see funeral arrangements."

She tossed the paper on the desk.

"So, what now?"

"What do you mean what now?"

"What are you going to do?"

"About what?"

"I can't believe you will sit here with the biggest murder case around here since who knows when and not stick your nose in it."

I picked up my drink and drained it. I raised my hand to throw it in the trash can.

"Don't even try," she said.

I smiled and did. The bottle bounced off the edge and fell to the floor. I'm glad the lid was on.

"You'll never learn," she said picking up the bottle and putting it where I couldn't.

"Do you have a funeral dress?" I asked.

"I wouldn't call it a funeral dress," she said returning to her seat, "but it's black. Are we going to a funeral?"

"I've seen that black dress."

"So."

"You're right it's not a funeral dress, but it will have to do."

There's that smile again.

"Why not go?" I said, "We could rub elbows with the rich and their groupies. We'll probably see a bunch of other businesspeople show their faces so people will think they care. There will be dignitaries from the city. You can bet the chief and the mayor will be there."

"Did you know the deceased?" Sheila smiled.

"No."

"AHA!" she said sitting up and slapped her hand on the desk. "I knew it."

"I never said I knew him."

"But you will stick your nose where it doesn't belong."

"I'll listen and maybe, just maybe, I might hear something."

"Well, we could use the business."

"That didn't cross my mind."

"Whatever. Don't you know Oliver Fletcher?"

"Yes," I said snapping my fingers, "and he may be there."

She got up and said, "I guess I better get back to pretending I'm working. I wouldn't want the boss to find out."

"What would he do if he did?"

She shrugged and went out, this time closing the door then immediately stuck her head in.

"Are you sure you don't want something to brighten up this drab office?"

"No, thanks. I'm happy with my stocking full of coal."

"Scrooge," she said and closed the door.

I went back to the window. Everything and everybody appeared to be back to normal and moving along smoothly. I didn't see any signs that anything out of the ordinary happened earlier.

I couldn't help but wonder if I was looking down on Barnett's killer. If he or she was good at it, they could move around like nothing happened carrying on their holiday chores. It was possible. When melancholy slips in this time of year, anything is possible. People kill others or kill themselves or both around Christmas. It seems to be a yearly tradition.

2

Tuesday, November 23rd

Edwin Barnett's funeral was the Tuesday before Thanksgiving. I pulled my old Chevy into the crowded parking lot and went straight to the back. I didn't want the highbrow cars scratching my classic 1964 Impala convertible.

Sheila's black dress fit her comfortably. She wore black shoes and carried a black purse. I thought it was a nice touch to match. I wore a not so new polo shirt, new black jeans, and loafers. Loafers are my shoes of choice when I'm dressed up. Today I wore socks even though it wasn't a formal affair.

We walked around the corner and faced a huge throng of people. I led Sheila through the horde to get inside. Many heads turned to look at her, or it might have been me. It was hard to tell.

The lobby was likewise full of people. Edwin Barnett was getting a rousing send off. The sign in the back looked like a directional signal with little arrows pointing two different directions. The guest of honor was lying in state in the large chapel. One of those state rooms wasn't large enough to accommodate one of Shelberg's prominent citizens.

"Looky, here, it's the poster boy for fashion."

I looked up from signing our condolences to see Oliver Fletcher, Ollie to most of his friends.

"Ollie," I said grabbing his hand, "fancy seeing you here."

He ignored me and turned to Sheila.

"You look ravishing, as usual, Sheila."

She did a little curtsy and smiled.

"Thank you," she said then nodded to me, "but he's a work in progress."

"He's been a work in progress for years. That your good clothes, Cameron?"

Ollie never would call me by my first name.

"I dressed up," I said. "I didn't want to stand out."

He looked me over.

"What are you doing here?"

"Yes, these are my good clothes, thank you and I'm, we, are here paying our respects."

"Did you know Mr. Barnett?"

"Not personally, but everybody knew of him and his family. What's the difference? He won't know who's here and who's not."

Ollie rubbed his chin, looked at me then at Sheila.

"It was his idea," she shrugged, "Business is slow."

"He'd come if your business was booming. He's after something, right, Cameron?"

"Okay, okay, enough about me," I said pulling them back as far as we could get, hugging the wall.

"What's going on, Ollie?"

"We're about to have a funeral."

"I gathered that much. I know you're on the case."

"Everybody does. It was in the paper."

"What can you tell me?"

"I can't tell you anything, Cameron. The investigation is in progress. That's all you need to know."

"You might want to tell him something," Sheila said, "even if it isn't true. It would soothe the savage beast."

Ollie shook his head and straightened his necktie. He was the neatest person I ever met.

"Look, Cameron, are you on the case? No, you're not, so I can't tell you anything even if there was something to tell which there isn't."

"Idle hands are the work of the devil," Sheila said, "He needs something to do."

Ollie looked around. No one was paying attention to us. I don't think they knew we were there.

"Listen," he whispered, "there's only one thing I can tell you and it better not get out."

I was licking my chops. Sheila smiled at my gluttony, but she wanted to know as much as I did only, she wasn't so obvious.

"If you tell anyone," He said pointing his finger in my face, "I'll take away all your Dr. Peppers."

I feigned panic.

"He's not on those anymore," Sheila said. "His doctor took him off. He's now a Diet Dr. Pepper addict."

"He's trying to save you from yourself, eh, Cameron? Well, good luck to him."

"Come on, Ollie," I said. "What gives?"

"The only thing missing was Barnett's cell phone. Just about everyone now a days has a cell phone so we will assume he also had one. A man like him probable does a lot of business on his phone. If we find it, we may be able to find the killer faster. He had a couple thousand dollars in his wallet. His office was neat as a pin except for the area around his desk. It was a bloody mess. Why would the killer only take the cell phone and leave that kind of cash? We got his secretary to come in and help us out. She couldn't find anything missing and she was baffled about the cell phone thing."

"Anybody call the cell phone?" I asked.

"Yes, she did while we were there, but no one answered."

I started to say something when we heard rumblings from the front of the lobby. We moved up to see what the commotion was. From outside in people parted like the Red Sea. I expected to see Moses.

Instead, a young woman dressed all in black wearing sunglasses made her way through. She didn't appear to be walking but gliding. It was also plain to see the designer didn't use a lot of material on her outfit. Two huge young men in dark suits flanked her and stayed close. They, too, wore sunglasses. They didn't bother to remove them once they were inside. Maybe they thought no one would recognize them.

She stopped when she got to us.

"You're not dressed for a funeral," she said.

I looked around.

"You talking to me?" I asked her.

"Yes."

"My regular funeral clothes are at the cleaners."

She pulled her glasses down to look over the top. My power of observation told me there were no bloodshot eyes. Not one tear in the corner of either eye. Maybe she would mourn later. I doubted it.

"What is your name?"

"Lee Cameron," I bowed, "at your service."

Sheila and Ollie tried to disassociate themselves from me, but the mass of people wouldn't let them move.

"The private detective?"

"That's what some people call me. I can't repeat the other names."

"I've heard of you."

"I'm sure it's all good, but don't believe most of it."

She turned to one of the hunks and whispered something. He looked at me and nodded. I felt I was about to get thrown out by the fashion police. She pushed her sunglasses back up and the entourage continued.

As the rest of the mourners passed us, Crystal Hudson walked by and winked at me.

"Bitch," Sheila whispered in my ear.

Sheila never missed an opportunity to complement Shelberg's number one reporter.

We followed and took a seat in the back of the chapel. The important mourners were up front.

After the minister finished the service, he called for anyone who would like to say a few words to come forward. Some people I assumed to be associates or business friends made little unimportant speeches. It struck me that their little antidotes were more for them than the dearly departed. Listening to all the praises heaped upon Barnett, I knew he was a wonderful man and would be missed. I wondered what kind of limo he would have waiting in the great beyond. Would it be white or red?

The multitude split up after a small gravesite ceremony. I walked to my car with Ollie and Sheila. One of Neda Barnett's young fellas was standing by my car.

"I know you can see it's a classic," I said walking up to him, "but it's not for sale no matter how much she wants to give me."

He didn't smile. I guess humor was against the rules. These type guys are always so serious. Maybe their jobs require it. If they smile, it could be construed as not taking their jobs serious.

"Mrs. Barnett wants to meet with you," he said.

"Which one?"

"Mrs. Neda Barnett."

He didn't say Mrs. Edwin Barnett. She had some independence. At least she did now.

"Why? Did she like my clothes?"

Ollie came by and patted me on the shoulder.

"I'm out of here before this gets really ugly."

He turned to Sheila.

"Do you need a ride?"

"No," she said, "but thank you. I'll see how this plays out."

"Tell her I can't today," I said to him. "I'm busy."

"Do you have a business card?"

I fished out my wallet and pulled out a folded card and handed it to him.

"My new set hasn't come in yet."

He looked at it then said, "Someone will be in touch," then walked off giving Sheila a good look in passing.

"She may want to hire you?"

"That or she wants fashion tips."

"I'd go with wanting to hire you."

"Hey, Cameron!"

I turned to see Crystal closing ranks on us. Sheila rolled her eyes.

"What's up, Crystal?" I asked.

"Hi, Sheila," she said extending her hand. Sheila gave her the old limp hand but didn't say anything.

"You on the Barnett case?" she asked turning back to me.

I looked at Sheila. She shook her head.

"What makes you think that?"

"I saw you talking to Neda Barnett and Oliver Fletcher at the funeral."

"I was paying my respects to Mrs. Barnett, and I've known Ollie Fletcher for years."

"Okay, Cameron," she said, "I'll find out. Bye."

"Hold it," I said, "Did you see Yvonne Barnett?"

"Yes, why?"

"Look."

Yvonne and Neda were off to the side away from the dispersing crowd. Yvonne was really giving it to her daughter-in-law, punctuating the air with her finger. Neda didn't respond other than the occasional nod.

"I can tell you one thing," Crystal said, "Yvonne turned beet red when she saw what Neda was wearing. She wrung her hands like she would like to have them around her cute little daughter-in-law's neck."

Yvonne slapped Neda across the face. The meeting broke up when Neda stormed off.

"Bye," Crystal said running after one of the combatants.

"Look over there," Sheila said when she turned away from watching Crystal.

Four women in black stood off to the side each holding a single flower. When the way cleared, they went to the casket and in turn each laid her flower on it. They left together.

"Come on," Sheila said getting in on her side of the car, "Let's go see Tom."

"My thoughts exactly."

We drove on a while before she spoke.

"How did you meet Oliver Fletcher?" she asked.

"I'll tell you if tell me why you dislike Crystal Hudson."

"Dislike? I never said I disliked her; I hate her, but okay. We'll trade stories."

"Ollie was a patrolman when I came out of the academy. They put me with him. We got to be friends, but we found out, as time went on, our police methods were different. At first, I followed his lead. I did everything he told me and showed me. After a while, I started to rebel, I guess you could call it. Normal police channels moved to slow. It would take forever to get the bad guys to trial. And when, or I should say if, they were found guilty, they'd get suspended sentences and were back on the street. We'd arrest them and the cycle would start all over. We arrested some so often we knew them by their first names."

"Did you think you could be the Dirty Harry type?" she asked.

"Not that drastic, but I wavered a little from regular police methods. Ollie told me about a hundred times to get back in line, but I kept on with my juvenile ways. Jack Vincent finally got involved and nailed my ass to the wall. I got suspended so many times; I finally said to hell with it and got out. No love lost on either side. Anyway, I stayed friends with Ollie. To be honest I got to the point where I missed police work. I knew I wasn't going back to the force, so I started this thriving agency you see before you."

"How long were you on the force?"

"Four years, maybe five. I don't remember. I do remember the last two were rough. I was running around like a crazy vigilante. Even the crooks complained about me. Imagine that. These guys were running around stealing, mugging, doing anything they could get away with and they were complaining about me being too rough."

I slapped the steering wheel for emphasis.

"Anyway," I said, "I was off the force and unemployed. I managed to scrape up some money to start this little venture."

Sheila didn't say anything about her story. I thought maybe she changed her mind. While waiting for her I thought how I did miss police work. I wasn't really just telling her that. I don't think I could go back to the force as long as Vincent was chief, but I would if it came up just the same.

"Why do you like Crystal Hudson so much?" she finally asked.

"I don't like her so much like you say. She hasn't done anything to me. A reporter can be a good source of information if you stay on her good side. What gives between you two?"

She sighed and looked out the window probably trying to decide if she made the right decision to tell me.

"Look," I said, "if you don't want to tell me, that's okay."

"No, we made a deal. It was back when we were in college. We were friends then, or we were working on a friendship. At least we got along. We had a history class together and there was a guy in this class. I—"

"Hold it," I said, "is this going to be about you two fighting over this guy?"

"The guy came between us, but not like you think?"

"Does this guy have a name?"

"Yes, but for the sake of this tale, he will remain anonymous."

"Okay, sorry, go on."

"We didn't know him that well, just from the class. We started hanging around together, you know, it all started at trying to be friends. Well, as it happens a lot of times, things started to get serious between me and the guy. Crystal didn't like it. She didn't say so, but I think she felt like the odd woman out. She told me this guy was bad news."

"How could she tell?"

"I don't know. She told me to stay away from him. She said she had a feeling. I couldn't see it or wouldn't. I thought she told me that because she wanted him. We got into a shouting match. I called her everything under the sun and that pretty much ended our short friendship. One night the guy and I were at his apartment, the first mistake. He made certain remarks and gestures that we should go in the bedroom. It was tempting because the guy was gorgeous. He had blond hair, blue eyes, and a body that wouldn't quit. I refused. He acted like no girl every turned him down. He persisted. When that didn't work, he put his hands all over me trying to get my clothes off. I fought him as best I could, but he was bigger and stronger. He finally figured out this wasn't going to be easy for him. Then he got mad and knocked me around. He was no dummy. He hit and kicked me in the back, in the stomach, legs, ribs, where you couldn't see. That really hurt, Lee…"

I hadn't realized it, but I had stopped the car in the middle of the street and stared at her. She was crying.

"Shelia, I—"

She held up her hand.

"No, let me finish and you better get going."

The honking behind me helped to get me started.

"Anyway, I managed to get a chair in his way and ran out the door. The only place I could think of going to was Crystal's. My whole body hurt, and I didn't know if I could even drive, but I wasn't staying around there. She opened the door after some begging on my part and I fell into her arms. She helped me sit down. I told her what happened. Instead of giving me the sympathy I expected from a friend, she vented on me. She told me everything that was wrong with me and with him and wanted to know why in the hell I didn't listen to her from the beginning. She said I was stupid for getting involved with him. She went on until I managed to stand. I slapped her across the face and called her egotistical bitch. She pushed me to the door, opened it, and told me to deal with it myself. I sat in my car and cried, full of self-pity."

I pulled into the parking lot and killed the engine.

"She's obviously past it," I said looking at her.

She wiped her eyes and straightened her hair.

"I suppose so."

"I didn't think—"

"How were you to know? I need to get over it, too, but when I think about how she went on and I was hurting. She was supposed to be my friend."

"Did you get involved with anyone else like that?"

"Not until I got married, but that was a few years after this happened."

I'd seen so much crap on how people treat each other, this type of thing wouldn't normally bother me. I felt for her. I was shaken by her story. It could have been because it was her and we were close. It wasn't a situation I could remove myself from like I was still on the street. I didn't know their names, but I hated them.

"I'm sorry, Sheila."

"Don't be, Lee. It's not your nature. Let's go in."

Tom was Tom Jones. He owned a sports bar called The 10th Inning. The clientele was mixed: doctors, college students, lawyers, construction workers, older folks. It was a good place to unwind and that's what we intended to do, especially after her story.

Tom was a former baseball player. He played some major league ball, but his career mostly confined to the minors. He had the place decorated in baseball gear and pictures of present and past players. Scattered throughout were framed newspaper articles which I never took time to read. During baseball season all his televisions were on either professional or college games and the Little League World Season when it was on.

We took a seat at the U-shaped bar. He waved and came over to us. He grabbed my hand and shook it vigorously then he leaned across the bar and kissed Sheila on the cheek.

Tom was trim and fit at fifty. He serves as owner, manager, bartender, and when the need arises, bouncer, but I've never seen any real problems in here.

"I see you have your funeral clothes on," he laughed. "How was it?"

"It was a funeral," I said, "so I guess it went okay as funerals go."

Tom wiped the bar. He was always wiping the bar.

"What'll you have?"

"Beer," Sheila said, "a big one."

"Dr. Pepper," I said.

"Come on, Lee, you know I don't carry Dr. Pepper. How about a coke?"

"He really means Diet Dr. Pepper," Sheila said.

"On the wagon, huh?" Tom said continuing to wipe the bar.

"Maybe I need to find another place to patronize."

"Right, I'll be right back."

He came back with our drinks and put them on coasters.

"A man after my own heart," Sheila smiled.

Tom flipped his towel over and said, "Well, what's the latest on Edwin Barnett's death?"

"Don't know," I said forcing down the coke, "but Ollie's on the case."

I contorted my face.

"Please," Sheila said, "quit acting like you're drinking poison."

"Good," Tom said, "Maybe he'll get a promotion out of it."

"He did say—"

"No," Sheila said wagging her finger in my face, "Oliver said it was hush hush."

"Hush hush?" Tom said, "I been knowing Ollie since before he got on the force."

"He told us the only thing missing was Barnett's cell phone."

Sheila shook her head.

"You couldn't keep your mouth shut if your life depended on it."

"You might want to use a different cliché," I said.

Tom laughed.

"You two sound like you're married."

I paid for the drinks, and we headed out. When I opened the door, the four ladies in black walked in. Being the gentleman, I held it open for them and watched until they found a table.

Sheila saw I had the urge to talk to them and grabbed my arm.

I saw Tom walking over to them as the door shut in my face.

"Was that the same group at the cemetery?" I said.

"It could be coincidence," Sheila said leaning her head back. "You know… four women in black running around together."

"Right. I should have talked to them."

"Why?"

"To find out why they're travelling as a group."

"Maybe they're on a Johnny Cash Memorial Tour."

"No," I said not catching her joke. "That's too far."

"You ever think they might like their privacy?"

"I guess it slipped my mind."

"You ever think that it may be none of your business?"

"You have all the answers, don't you?"

"Not all just more than you."

She smiled and closed her eyes.

I drove on without a word, but my wheels were turning. I'd find some way to get in on this case.

3

Tuesday, November 30th

The last day of November was wet. Depressing for some, but not for me. I like rain. It makes being inside cozy. I stood at the window sipping my breakfast watching the shoppers contend with the elements. I wondered what happened to the grandma and the mugger who attacked her. I smiled at the thought of Granny cleaning his plow.

I didn't see any funny business in my little area of vision. It was out there. You could bet on it. There's all kinds of funny business going on this time of year. The teen mugger is the enemy; grandma is the heroine. Their incidence is just the tip of the holiday crime iceberg.

Sheila would want to go shopping eventually braving the elements and not giving a second thought to the idiocy.

The phone rang in Sheila's office.

"Today?" I heard her say. "Now?"

She came in and stood next to me.

"Friendly call?" I asked.

"Neda Barnett is on her way over here now. She insisted."

"She's probably used to getting her way. She's from the "I married a rich old man" generation. Even if you told her no, she would show up anyway."

I finished off my drink and tossed the bottle at the can. I missed.

"No use having these scattered around the office with her highness coming," she said picking up the bottle. "What would she think?"

I shrugged.

"I hate her," Sheila said.

"You hate everybody."

"I don't hate you."

"I'm working on it."

"I better get out there," she said motioning to her office." I would hate for Mrs. Barnett to face an empty office."

"Leave the door open."

Sheila went to her desk, and I went back to watching the crowd.

Then I noticed another would-be young mugger. These kids weren't the smartest in the world. Why wouldn't they wait for dark when it would easier? Unless they ran into another grandma.

I heard the outer office door open then close. No words spoken. Neda Barnett barged past Sheila without a word and came into my office.

I didn't say anything but concentrated on the teen robber waiting for a victim.

"Mr.—" she started.

I held up my hand. I could hear her tapping her foot in frustration for having to wait. I bet she had her arms crossed. The kid decided the time wasn't right and walked away.

"Mrs. Barnett," I said walking to her, "Please sit down."

She sat in one of the chairs reserved for clients across from my desk. I walked over and shut the door. I could see why dear old mother-in-law was upset at how she dressed at the funeral. It was the same here. She was ready and willing to show off her assets.

"Mrs. Barnett," I said sitting at the desk, "we have rules in this office. It was rude of you to walk in here ignoring my secretary. It shows bad manners and I'm sure it won't happen again."

"Mr. Cameron, I'm not in the mood for your—"

I held up my hand.

"Mrs. Barnett, I don't know why you're here, but we will have manners in here or you can get your ass out of my office."

I got up and went to the frig.

"Something to drink? I have Diet Dr. Pepper and, uh…that's it."

"No thanks."

I went back to my desk and made sure I put the bottle on the coaster.

"No one talks to me like that," she said.

"I'm sure. No one just barges into my office, either. Why are you here?"

"I want you to find out who killed my husband."

"I'm not in the habit of finding killers. My job is a little bit more low key. You know, staking out houses, watching for cheating husbands and wives or locating missing people who don't want to be found. That kind of stuff."

"Are you afraid?"

"You damn right I'm afraid. I don't want people shooting at me any more than you would, and you don't need to test my manhood."

I took a sip and waited for her to speak. She didn't.

"Isn't that the police's job?"

"Yes, but I prefer someone I can trust."

"What makes you think you can trust me more than the police?"

"I know your reputation. I checked you out."

"And you still trust me?"

"Can we cut the comedy?"

I shrugged. The woman had no sense of humor. I probably wouldn't either if I just lost my bank account, especially one that big.

"Okay, but before I decide, we need to discuss matters."

"What kind of matters?"

I took out a legal pad and pen. It makes me look important.

"Do you know who might want to kill your husband?"

"No."

"Is there anyone he had a disagreement with?"

"Not that I can think of."

"Did he make a deal with anyone, and have it turn sour?"

"My husband was a businessman, a very wealthy businessman. He made deals, as you say, all the time. I'm sure not all worked out in his favor."

I tapped the pen on the pad.

"Obviously someone wanted him dead. Think, Mrs. Barnett."

I could see her brain working to come up with names. I sipped and waited.

"Isaac Kruger."

"The attorney?"

"None other."

Isaac Kruger was head of the largest law firm in town. He catered mainly to wealthy clients and usually won his case. He was big, loud, and intimidated witnesses and jurors. Some say he could intimidate the judge.

"Why do you think Kruger would want to kill your husband?"

"They were friends once. Kruger did some work for Edwin."

"Business or personal?"

"Both, but I think it was the personal end that broke up the relationship."

"Do you know what it was about?"

"No."

"But you might think it was bad enough for someone in Kruger's position to risk everything to kill your husband."

"You asked for a name, and I gave you one."

"Right, but I want legitimate names, not something you'll throw out to pacify me."

I wanted to reach across that desk and grab her by the throat, but I wrote Kruger's name instead.

"Did your husband carry on his personal business at home?"

"Some, I think."

"Would the staff be privy to anything?"

"No. Why would they be?"

"You never know what they might overhear."

"If I or my husband were to catch them eavesdropping, they would be terminated on the spot."

"I'm sure they would.

And they would be drawn and quartered or tarred and feathered or both.

"Anyone else?"

"How many do you need?"

I put the pen down and folded my hands on the desk.

"Look, Mrs. Barnett, I'm not looking for a certain number of names. I need the names of those who you think might want to kill your husband. That could be one name, two names, or twenty. We need a starting point. Understand?"

"Yes," she said taking a pack of cigarettes out of her purse.

"You mind?" she said starting to light up.

"Not in my office."

The motion to her mouth stopped. I'm sure the question was a formality, but she put in back in her purse.

"Now," I said, "who else?"

"Philo Griggs."

"Are you sure?"

"Yes. He worked for my husband for a while. He was angry when Edwin fired him."

Philo Griggs was a Parade All-American tackle in high school. For those of you not familiar with football, it means he would be one of the most sought-after players by the major colleges. Some of the biggest football factories courted him. Then in the third to last week of the season, he tore up his knee. The big guys couldn't get out of town fast enough. The only school willing to take a chance on him was local Shelberg College.

That would have been okay. He could still prove he was good enough to play in the NFL, but Philo had one problem. Like a lot of players, college was just a place to showcase his talent, but he wouldn't or couldn't cut it in the classroom and flunked out. He picked up odd jobs around town. When they didn't pay enough, he graduated to drugs and small crimes. Most thought he got out of those jams because of who he was. Edwin Barnett obviously didn't play that game.

"What kind of work did he do?" I asked.

"Handy man, yard work, repairs, things like that."

"Why did he get fired?"

"He was stealing from us. By the time we found out, he had stolen and sold thousands of dollars worth of equipment plus he was using drugs on the property."

"Was he dealing drugs?"

"We never found out."

"And Mr. Barnett prosecuted him."

"Yes. Edwin didn't think firing him was enough. My husband actually liked Philo Griggs. He thought sending him to prison might straighten him out. Anyway, when they sent him off, he swore to my husband he would get even when he got out.”

"Do you really think he did it?”

“I don’t know.”

I wrote Griggs’ name below Kruger’s.

“Anyone else?”

“No.”

“How did Mr. Barnett get along with his mother?”

“He did whatever she wanted.”

“She wasn’t too happy with him for marrying you, was she?”

Neda fidgeted in her chair. I knew she wanted a smoke.

“What does that have to with this?”

“It may have a lot to do with everything or it may mean nothing. I need to touch all the bases. Only time will tell.”

“No, she wasn’t happy about Edwin marrying me. She didn’t want him to have a wife young enough to be his daughter. Is that what you want me to say?”

“Not necessarily.”

I took a sip and returned the bottle to its proper place.

“Can we get on with it?” she said.

“There’s a name missing here.”

“Who’s?”

“Yours.”

She jumped up, lost her balance, and almost fell over. She quickly rectified her situation but tipped the chair backwards.

“MINE!?”

“Yes, yours, please sit down.”

When it was apparent, I was not going to help her, she righted the chair and sat down.

“How can you be so bold as to accuse me?”

“Let me explain something to you,” I said emptying the bottle. I replaced the cap and tossed it. I missed.

“A young wife married to an older wealthy man will be the prime suspect—”

I pointed my finger at her.

"—and the cops will look really hard at you until they are satisfied you didn't do it. And you can be sure of one more thing. Did Mr. Barnett have a life insurance policy?"

"Yes."

"How much?"

"Does it matter?"

"It may when it comes to motive."

"I believe it's around five million dollars."

I had to take the figure in before I could go on then wrote it down.

"The insurance company will have their own investigation before paying you one red cent. They want to be sure there was no foul play on your part."

She said nothing.

"Have you ever had an affair since you've been married to Mr. Barnett?"

She hesitated.

"Your hesitation to answer could be construed as a yes."

"I have not. I've always been true to Edwin."

I tapped my finger on the pad then added her name to the other two.

"You'd be wise to get an attorney," I said.

"Why?"

"Like I said, the cops will be looking at you first. The insurance company and I'm sure Yvonne Barnett will try to find whatever dirt she can on you. An attorney can guide you through the rough spots."

"Now that you've asked me everything that could humiliate me," she said digging in her purse, "will you take my case?"

"Yes, I will," I said taking a contract from the drawer, "but I want to make something clear. I will not put up with any interference from you or anyone associated with you. I won't make any deals. Here's the most important thing. If I find out you've been lying to me about anything, I'll drop you like the proverbial hot potato and work to have your ass thrown in jail."

I stood and put out my hand.

"If you agree to all this, we have a deal."

She stood and took my hand. If her eyes were guns, I'd be dead.

"Please give this to my secretary and I'll get started."

I handed her the contract.

"Mrs. Barnett," I said when she reached my office door.

"Yes," she said without turning around.

"I don't really believe you did it and I don't believe Kruger or Griggs did it either, but I'll talk to them. They may be able to tell us something. It won't hurt to try, and it gives us a place to start."

Then she turned to face me.

"I hope you're as good as I've heard," she said, turned, and walked out.

I heard some talking in the outer office but didn't hear anything resembling an altercation. Then the door opened and shut. Sheila came in.

"Do you think Miss Fancy Pants did it?" she asked after depositing the bottle in its rightful place.

"No."

"Why?"

"What would she gain? I'm willing to bet old Edwin dished out a good allowance to her. She comes and goes like she wants to. It appears he didn't put any restrictions on her."

"What about a young hunk? She could meet him on one of her trips. I'll bet she's lying about an affair."

Neda Barnett takes a trip out of the country once a month. The paper covered her jaunts, but nothing illegal or immoral ever made the news.

"Possibly but think about this. She told me his life insurance is around five mil. She could make a lot more than that if she stays with him. She kills him or has him killed then she goes to prison and gets nothing, but plenty of good loving every night. If she had a guy stashed, it would be wise to keep him stashed."

"Good loving every night," she smiled, "you're so crude."

"It's the way I am and that's the way it is."

I handed her the pad.

"What do you know about these names?"

Sheila made a quick glance over the names.

"She thinks they did it?"

"She was throwing names out. I can't fathom Isaac Kruger killing Barnett. Griggs might want to. Barnett hauled his ass into court when he caught Griggs stealing equipment from him."

Sheila tossed the pad on the desk.

"Why don't we go see Tom and let Neda Barnett treat us to lunch?" I asked heading for the door.

The 10th Inning was packed like I figured it would be. We sat at the bar. All the televisions had shows reliving the previous week's games.

"Well, what do I owe the honor?" Tom smiled.

For once he had the towel slung across his shoulder.

"We're celebrating," I said.

"Oh, yeah, what's the occasion?"

The towel was out and he was wiping the cleanest bar in town. Then he stopped.

"You two getting married?"

"No," Sheila said, "Neda Barnett hired Lee."

Tom shook both our hands.

"I'm sure you'll find out who did it if you can stay out of jail yourself," he said to me.

"How about lunch?" Sheila asked.

I ordered a roast beef po-boy, no pickles please. Sheila ordered the same thing with everything just to show me how tough she was. We ate in silence splitting our time listening to the shows and the drone of the crowd.

"How was it?" Tom asked.

"Great, as usual," Sheila said, "and the pickles were delicious."

"Good, I like a satisfied customer."

"You ever see Isaac Kruger or Philo Griggs in here?" I asked.

Tom shook his head.

"That's something," he said. "I get a mix of clientele, rich, poor, middle class. They mingle. No problem. Kruger's too big a shot to come in here. You think I'd try and poison the guy. I thought Griggs was in prison."

"He's out."

"What's with them?"

"They're my first two suspects."

"Yeah?" Tom smiled. "What an odd couple. I want to see you pin this on Kruger."

"If he did it," I said paying Tom, "I'll get him."

"Yeah, Lee, somehow I think you will."

He turned to walk away then came back.

"Listen, Lee. You be careful out there. Anyone willing to kill a rich guy like Edwin Barnett won't have a problem killing you."

He looked at Sheila.

"You watch out for him. You know he does some crazy stuff."

I rolled my eyes.

"Well, I appreciate your concern, Tom, but it's getting a little mushy in here for me."

He nodded, patted my shoulder, and went back to his other customers.

"Tom!" I called.

He came back.

"What about the ladies in black?"

"Not much. They talked about general stuff as far as I could tell."

"Didn't give away why they were all in black?"

"No, but when I got to their table, they quit talking. The only thing they said when I was there was their orders."

"Thanks, Tom."

He looked at Sheila then back at me.

"Are these women in your future?"

"Possibly. They were at the funeral, then they were here. Makes it interesting."

He nodded and left.

I choked down my coke and we headed for the door.

Tom watched us like he didn't plan to see either of us again.

4

Wednesday, December 1st

I stood at the window drinking breakfast and watching the crowd below. The Christmas spirit abounded. Sheila put up a tree in her office, but I didn't want one in mine. She gave me a tee shirt with "Bah Humbug" on the front and "Please See Front" on the back. I wore it proudly.

The number of shoppers had grown. The sky and temperature were cooperating. The cool air made it feel like Christmas was indeed near. They moved with excited anticipation of the coming season, but not with the urgency that would come in the following weeks. They actually appeared to be having fun.

Edwin Barnett was buried and doing whatever it is one does in the afterlife. It was all over but finding the killer. I was preparing my plan of action and still trying to figure out why I took the case. It was just a matter of time before the cops found out and they would not look kindly on me.

Sheila tapped on my office door and stuck her head in.

"Jack Vincent wants to see you in his office right now."

Maybe the word was out already, and Jack Vincent wanted to ream me out. I wouldn't stop the cops from doing their part, but Jack might look at it as interfering. He also knew I had more leverage than your average everyday department detective. He kept them in line and by the book. I didn't have such hindrances.

I turned away from my entertainment.

"Did he say why?"

"I don't know. I'm not high enough on the food chain. Secretaries are like children; they want us seen and not heard."

"That's why I love you."

She went back to her office mumbling something I knew I was better off not understanding.

The Shelberg Central Police Station is just down the street from my office past the mayor and district attorney's offices and a Taco Bell. One day I would work up enough nerve to ask Jack why they didn't push for a donut shop instead of the Taco Bell. I decided to walk and jumped into the flowing river of shoppers. I put my bottle on Sheila's desk on the way out. She did another mumbling thing and tossed it into her trash basket. She never misses.

Jack Vincent is a forty-year veteran of the police department and it seemed like he'd been chief for ages. He and I didn't see eye-to-eye on how I should do my job, so I made an early exit from doing police work, at least on this police force. I didn't know why he wanted to see me, but I'd bet it wasn't his idea.

"Lee Cameron to see Chief Vincent," I said to the receptionist. "I know the way."

"Hold it," she said looking at her list. She checked my name off. "I'll show you to his office."

I shrugged and followed her. I guess they didn't trust me not to get lost.

When she opened the door to Jack Vincent's office, I was surprised to see the mayor and district attorney sitting side by side like they were the best of friends.

"Please sit down, Lee," Jack said. He hadn't lost any of his 240 pounds since I saw him at Barnett's funeral. His hair was thinning; his dark eyes showed signs of wear. Dealing with the criminal element for as long as he has would wear one thin, but not Jack.

"You know the mayor and district attorney, I assume," he said motioning in their direction.

"Yes," I said in my most polite manner, "good morning, ladies."

Melody Broussard accomplished two things when she won the mayor's race. She was not only the first female, but the first black mayor. She was in her third term because the people loved her. She won her last two re-election bids by wide margins. I thought she was an oddity for a politician: soft spoken and humble.

District Attorney Ursula Daniels was a different story. She was arrogant and thought the sun rose and set on her. She could battle any man in the courtroom and often won her convictions. One of her victims was Isaac Kruger and I doubt if he liked her.

"I'll get to the point, Lee," Jack said, "Yvonne Barnett came in here the other day. She wants this case cleared up quickly and quietly. She doesn't want the Barnett name dragged through the mud."

"I saw it in the paper," I said, "but I'd like to verify something. Is Ollie running the case?"

"Detective Fletcher is the lead investigator."

I sat silent waiting to hear what I already knew.

"Mr. Cameron," Ursula said, "Since Mrs. Barnett, the older one, is adamant about getting everything done as soon as possible, we feel you could help us."

"In what way?"

"I don't have to tell you I'm not a fan of your methods."

Jack sighed and wiped his balding head. Melody smiled and waited her turn.

"What methods are you talking about?" I asked.

"It seems that when you were with the department, you used, shall I say, unorthodox methods of arrests and interrogations."

"And my results?"

"Your results were commendable, but you left the department with a black eye more than once."

"Maybe the department should learn to defend itself."

I didn't like this woman, so it wasn't hard for her to get me riled.

"Did you call me in here to discuss my past? What's the point? What do you want?"

"Mr. Cameron," Melody jumped in at the appropriate time, "we'd like you to assist the department. It may speed up the process."

"What is it you want me to do?"

"We'd like you to work independent of the department," Jack said.

I shook my head and smiled.

"You mean you don't want me working directly with the cops so if I use my unorthodox methods, it can't be traced back."

"It would be nice," Ursula said, "if you could keep your investigations within the confines of the law."

"I'll do my best."

Melody smiled. Jack shook his head.

"Who do I report to?"

"Detective Fletcher," Jack said.

"Good, we work well together."

"You hand over whatever you find to Detective Fletcher."

"I will."

"There's one more thing," Ursula said.

There was always one more thing.

"We need to keep everything quiet. No media attention."

I shifted in my chair.

"How do you plan to do that?"

"That's up to you and Detective Fletcher."

"Fair enough."

I snapped my fingers like I just remembered something important.

"One more thing," I smiled, "Neda Barnett hired me today. It appears she has the same idea as you."

Ursula and Jack, ever so wary of things getting out of hand, could just look at each other. Melody maintained her smile.

"Is that a problem?" Ursula asked.

"Not to me so I now I have two people to report to."

"You are not to give her any information that would jeopardize the investigation."

"She's paying me a lot more money than you."

Jack wiped his head again then looked at the handkerchief. I didn't know what he expected to see.

"Just keep everything quiet, Lee, please," he pleaded. "If anything gets out that would, in her words, damage the Barnett name she'll have our heads."

"Not mine," I said, "it looks like big money is running this town. She has the three of you by the, er, well, you know. I'll run my investigation and I'll keep it quiet. If anything slips out, it won't be from me. How will you handle your press conferences?"

"What do you mean?" Jack asked.

"What will you tell the press? They won't settle for no comment."

"We'll take care of that," Ursula said.

She stood and put out her hand. I rose and took it.

"I hope we can work it out," she said.

She left without waiting for one of my witty retorts.

"Thank you," Melody said, "Ursula has her good points, but she can be a little abrupt."

"Thank you, Madam Mayor," I said bowing. "I'm sure we'll get this resolved in the manner prescribed by Mrs. Barnett."

She smiled and patted my cheek.

"I like you," she said and left.

"Sit down, Lee, for minute," Jack offered.

Jack Vincent had the look of someone who was on his last leg with the Shelberg Police Department. It wouldn't surprise me if he retired after they closed the books on this case.

"Do you know Crystal Hudson?" he asked.

"Yes."

"She's been snooping around. She's determined to find out more than we would like her to know. I cannot express how important secrecy is here."

"Like I said, I'll keep a lid on my end, but Crystal is a hound. She'll know something is up and she may dig enough to get more than you want her to."

"I know. There's not much we can do about that."

"You might want to try some kind of gag order."

"Then they'll really know something's up. No, we'll take our chances like it is."

He stood and put out his hand.

"No hard feelings about the past? What's done is done. Okay?"

"Okay, Chief," I said shaking his hand.

I walked out of his office to find Melody Broussard sitting on a bench in the hall.

"Mr. Cameron," she said getting up.

"Call me Lee."

She smiled.

"Did you wait for me?" I asked.

"Yes, I wanted to speak with you alone."

"I'm flattered."

"What you said in there about Yvonne Barnett running the town is not that far from the truth. The council, the chief, the DA are all running scared because of what she might do if things don't go her way."

"And what is her way?"

"She seems more concerned about how the family name will be affected more than finding out who killed her son. The image of the family and the company are most important. She donates money to the campaigns to all parties involved and they don't want that money to dry up. Maybe we didn't make ourselves clear in our little meeting. What Yvonne Barnett doesn't want is for you or the police to find anything on her son that would make him look less than immaculate. I hope you understand."

"I do, but you didn't include yourself in the running scared bunch."

"This is my last term. It's been fun and I met a lot of interesting people. I hope I accomplished what I set out to do, but I'm tired of the bureaucracy and the money mongers. Yvonne Barnett can do what she will. I'm done with it."

"The press will create something if they don't get the information they like which could be worse."

"I know. Yvonne Barnett can handle that too, if it comes down to that."

She put out her hand.

"It's been a pleasure talking to you, Lee. We appreciate your cooperation."

"I don't know about the "we" part," I smiled.

"Tell me one more thing," she said, "if you want to."

"Of course."

"Why did you take a murder case?"

"I was wondering that earlier and to tell you the truth, Madam Mayor, I don't really know. PIs don't normally go chasing after killers, but what the hell. Maybe it's the money. Neda Barnett is paying a tidy sum for me to find her husband's killer. It's like she wants me to beat the cops to it. I don't know. I'll try it and see what happens."

"I guess that will suffice."

"Does it sound crazy?"

She nodded and said, "No crazier than everything else going on."

"What do you mean by crazier?"

"The Christmas rush, Edwin Barnett getting killed, the Barnetts scrambling to find out who killed their master. Seems like everything is happening at the same time."

I walked the mayor to her building. She stopped along the way to greet passersby and shake their hands. It was an enjoyable walk.

I stopped in front of the bank building to watch the crowd. They were the same bustling, no time to lose multitude, but only up close. I didn't share their enthusiasm but admired their persistence. I watched until my view was blocked by a huge white pickup. It moved slow, the driver in no hurry. He looked around, but I could tell him he wouldn't find a parking place around here. Then he moved on. I smiled at the feasting swarm and went in.

The smile came off when I saw the frown on Sheila's face.

"What's up? What did I do?" I asked.

"You didn't do anything, but it's early."

She nodded toward my office.

"Who?" I asked stepping closer and lowering my voice.

"The bitch," she whispered.

According to Sheila, "bitch" could be any female of the human species.

I poked my head in ready to dodge a bullet or flying purse. Crystal Hudson sat across from my desk. I closed the door and went to the frig.

"Something to drink?"

"No thanks," she said.

I sat down, removed the cap, and took a long drink.

"Good stuff, Crystal, you should try it."

She just smiled.

"What brings you here?" I asked making sure I put the bottle on the coaster.

"You know why I'm here. What's up with Sheila? She acts like she hates me."

"She told me the story about you two. She hasn't gotten over it. Besides she hates everybody, but me."

"She does need to get over it and quit being so juvenile," she said taking out her little tape recorder, "you working the Barnett case?"

"You can put that thing away. Everything we say is off the record."

"The people have—"

"The people have nothing to do with it. It's you, Crystal. The people will find out in time. You're acting like a ball hog. Now the recorder goes, or you do."

She pretended to pout but put it back in the large bag she always dragged around.

"Why is it off the record?"

"First, I want to be sure you understand when I say off the record, that's what I mean. You don't print anything we say here…nothing. Understand?"

"Yes."

"Good."

I took another drink.

"What do you know?" I asked.

"Not much."

"You must know something. You were at the funeral and like me you weren't there to pay your respects. Then you just show up here at the same time I'm in Jack Vincent's office. Come on, Crystal."

"I don't know more than you. I can't get anyone to talk."

"That could be because Yvonne Barnett met with the chief, the mayor, and the DA. She flashed her wallet around and told them to get this thing finished quickly and quietly with the accent on quietly. And quickly, but mostly quietly."

"Maybe she thinks…or knows her little boy was not an angel."

"Could be. She doesn't want the good Barnett name tarnished."

"The company will move on. Killing the main man won't stop that if that was the killer's intension."

"I don't believe anyone would be that dumb, but you never know."

"You working on the case?"

"I'm working independently."

"What about Neda Barnett?"

"What about her?"

"She came in here. She hire you?"

"Did you see her come in here or into the building?"

"The building, but I'll bet my job she came to talk to you."

I finished the drink, put the cap on and started to toss it, but put it down.

"She seems to think more eyes on the target the better."

She took a deep breath, frustrated.

"She gave me a couple of names to check out," I said.

"Who?" she said leaning forward.

"Can't say. It's the old client detective code of secrecy. You have the same rules."

"That's true."

"You can't give me your sources. I can't give you the names."

"We could work together."

"I work alone."

She nodded toward the outer office.

"What about Miss Sourpuss out there. What does she know?"

"You two need to mend your fences."

"We'll work on it if she's up to it. Now, what does she know?"

"She may know more than me. She's not talking either."

"Look, Lee, the rich die, too and when they do it's big news especially when it's murder. Why so quiet?"

"Because Yvonne Barnett can make a lot of trouble if she wants."

"Sounds like she's running the show."

"Money talks and…you know the rest."

"What about what I find out on my own?"

"I have no control over that, but you need to be careful. I'm sure Barnett's companies spend a lot on advertising with the paper."

"I'm sure they do," she shrugged.

"If she doesn't like what she reads, it could be costly for the paper."

"I run everything by my boss before it goes in."

"Still, she can make it hard on the top dogs. Better be careful with this one, Crystal. That kind of money plays a game only they can win. You get some dirt on the good Edgar Barnett and print it; Yvonne Barnett could have your job."

"I'll be as careful as I need to be."

"It's your job and your ass."

Curiosity got the best of me, so I tossed the bottle at the can. No dice. Sheila came in, picked it up, gave us a dirty look, and left with the bottle in her hand. She must have been waiting for an opportunity or reason to come in my office.

"On second thought," I said, "maybe we can work together."

That perked her up.

"How?"

"You don't print anything until I tell you."

"Only if I get it first and you give me time to get it in."

"Deal. You run what you find by me, first. We may be able to work it where we can flush the killer out."

"You mean with bogus information."

"We'll work it out as we go."

"Okay. Who do you think killed Barnett?"

"Off the record. Remember?"

"Yes," she said leaning forward waiting for me to say something groundbreaking.

"The person who killed Edwin Barnett is—"

I looked around to make sure we were alone.

"—is someone who didn't like him."

She leaned back and sighed.

I snapped my fingers.

"I have something you can do."

She had lost her enthusiasm.

"What?"

"You ever go to The 10th Inning?"

"That watering hole for frustrated sports dropouts?"

"Hey! I go there."

"I rest my case."

"Okay," I shrugged, "I wouldn't want to put you out. Forget it."

"Don't give me that crap. You know I'll go for a story."

"The guy who owns the place is named Tom Jones."

"You're kidding."

"I wouldn't lie."

"Tom Jones the book, Tom Jones the singer, and now Tom Jones the sports bar owner."

"I didn't name him."

"Go on."

"You come to me before you print what you find."

"But you said I could print whatever I come up with."

"I put you on to this so it's not really yours."

"Okay, okay."

"I saw four women at the graveyard. They were dressed in black."

"I saw them but didn't pay attention."

"I'm surprised at you, Crystal. Didn't you notice they stood off to the side and didn't go to the casket until everyone else left?"

She shrugged.

"Well, Miss Sourpuss and I went to Tom's place after the funeral. Those women came in just as we were leaving. See if you can find out anything."

She let out another sigh but agreed.

"Is that all?" she asked standing.

"That's it. Do we have a deal?"

"Okay, but I get first crack at everything. Remember?"

"I remember."

She went to the door and turned.

"Do you know when Neda Barnett's next trip out of town is?"

"No."

"I'll see what I can find out," she said, smiling.

I nodded and she left.

Sheila was on me in a flash still holding the bottle.

"Well, what did she want?"

"She wanted to know what was going on. She's a reporter. That's her job."

Sheila sat across from me tapping the bottle on her knee.

"What did Jack Vincent want?"

"They want me to work with them."

"They?"

"Yeah, the chief, the mayor and the DA. Yvonne Barnett's on their asses."

"What did you tell them?"

"I told them yes."

"When do we start?"

"We? What's this we crap?"

"I want to go with you when you start beating the suspects with a rubber hose."

"That's only in movies and dark back rooms."

"I want to go."

"Why?"

"I'm tired of sitting in here. It gets boring."

"It's your job. Besides, it could be dangerous."

"I can take care of myself."

"You know how big Griggs is? Can you defend yourself against him? I'd have my hands full just fighting him off much less trying to protect you."

"Don't flatter yourself. I don't plan on fighting anyone. I just want to watch you work."

She tossed the bottle in the can. Nothing but net.

"Look," she said, "if it gets too dangerous, I'll back off and you can go on in your manly manner."

"You sure know how to make a guy feel good about himself."

"Come on, Lee. You know you'll give in. Why all the fuss?"

She was right. I'm a wimp when it comes to her.

She smiled.

"Now, when do we start?"

"Tomorrow. I'm going to talk to Ollie to get caught up. Find out who Philo Griggs' parole officer is. We'll start with him after I talk to Ollie."

"Anyone talk to his secretary yet?"

"I don't know, but I'll check with Ollie."

"She may know a lot more than anyone thinks."

"You're right."

She nodded and left.

I went back to the window. If the multitude down there thought about Edwin Barnett, it was pushed from their minds. Shelberg's most prominent citizen was my, and the police's, business now.

I looked at the cloudless sky and thought it was much too beautiful to hunt down a killer.

5

Thursday, December 2nd

I got to the police station around eight am. Ollie was standing at the receptionist desk.

"Our helper has arrived," he said to the receptionist. "You better watch this one. He doesn't play well with others…and please don't feed him. If you do, you'll never be rid of him."

"I know I can always depend on you, Ollie."

"Good morning," I said to the girl who had escorted me to the chief's office. "Ollie's always trying to boost my ego."

"Like you need help," he said, "come on."

We went back to this office. It was as neat as he is. There was an even stack of files on one corner of his desk. He motioned to a chair.

"Congrats," he said, "on getting thrown into the fire."

We shook hands and I sat.

"Looks like Old Lady Barnett has her claws bared," I said.

"Yeah," he said taking the top file and opening it.

"What do you have so far?" I asked.

"Edwin Barnett was shot in the stomach. Blood all over the place where we found him. The guy was probably in a lot of pain until the end. We believe he was standing up when he was shot because if he was sitting and leaning over on his desk the bullet couldn't have reached where it did."

He turned a page.

"This happened around ten the night of November 17th. Everyone else was gone from the building. I doubt if anyone in the vicinity, if there was anyone, would hear anything."

"The paper said his secretary called it in?"

"Yes. When she went in the following morning, she saw his car there earlier than usual. She knocked on his office door. When he didn't answer, she said she knocked again. When he still didn't answer, she went in and found him slumped over the desk."

"Was she in any kind of shock or panic?"

"No. According to the 911 operator she was calm. There was no hysterics or even crying."

"You ever find his phone?"

"No and that's the strange part. He had all this cash on him, and the killer only takes the phone."

"How do you know it was the killer?"

Ollie leaned forward and frowned at me.

"Who else would it be?"

"I don't know, but it seems the killer would have gone through his pockets and desk to find something of value."

"Maybe our killer is not a thief, just a killer."

"If he took the phone, he's a thief."

Ollie nodded.

"You talk to his secretary?" I asked.

"Yeah, but we didn't get much out of her. Just what I told you."

"You mind if I try? She could be our best link."

"Why do you say that?"

"Secretaries, as I am told by someone who pointed it out to me, know a lot more about their bosses than they let on. If nothing else, I'll see if what she tells me matches what she told you."

He waved his hand.

"Go ahead."

"What about the crime scene?"

"Nothing messed up other than the area where he was killed. He must have tried to do some other things because it looked like he was reaching around the desk. Blood was on his office phone and the little nooks where you can stash notes and letters and such."

"Maybe he was trying to find something to leave a message for someone. Maybe he knew his killer."

Ollie turned to another sheet and scratched his head.

"There was another strange thing."

"What?"

"He looked like he was smiling. When the officer answering the call arrived and found him after the secretary called it in. He said Edwin Barnett had a smile on his face. Why would he smile when he knew he was dying?"

"Like you said, he probably knew his killer. He was trying to find a way to let us know who he was. Or she. The smile was to let us know he knew something we didn't, but the smile goes to the grave with him. We won't really know why."

"I don't think I would smile if I was dying."

"Maybe not. What's his secretary's name?"

"Doreen Tilly."

"Right, now I remember. It was in the paper."

"What kind of gun?"

"A hunting rifle if you want to believe that."

It was time for me to lean forward.

"You mean this guy walks into Barnett's office with a rifle? Why a rifle? A handgun would have been so much easier and easier to hide."

"You think it's a man?"

"I would think so. I can't picture a woman bringing a rifle to a murder. I picture a woman with a handgun, but a lot of women hunt these days. So, to keep our options open, let's assume it could be either."

"Maybe our killer didn't care if Barnett saw the gun. He, or she, meant to kill him. I don't believe it's a robbery gone bad. This, uh, person intended on murder going in."

"What else about the crime scene?" I asked.

"Like I said, we think he was standing when he was shot. The bullet went through him and left a nasty exit wound. It went through the back of the chair and lodged in the wall behind his chair. We dug it out and sent it to ballistics."

I stood and walked around the room.

"What do you know about Isaac Kruger and Philo Griggs?"

"Kruger's a big-name attorney. If I remember right, he used to do work for Barnett. I heard they had a falling out and Barnett severed the deal. Griggs is out of prison working at the docks, I believe. Why?"

"Neda Barnett hired me."

"Lucky you."

"When I asked her if she might know someone who would want to kill her husband, she gave those two names."

"Kruger would be a long shot, but it's possible. With his ego, he probably didn't take to kindly to Barnett canning him, but I don't think he'd resort to murder. He could find a better way to retaliate if that's what he wanted. Griggs is a different story. Hot shot football player gone bad."

"Neda Barnett told me her husband fired him for stealing equipment then doing drugs on their property. Barnett prosecuted him and off he went. He said he'd get even when he got out of prison."

Ollie shook his head.

"I don't believe it's Kruger. If it's Griggs, he'd have additional problems with having a firearm by a convicted felon, but that would be the least of his worries."

"I'll give Doreen Tilly another shot, pardon the pun. Maybe she remembered something since you talked to her. Sheila's checking on Griggs' parole officer. I plan to talk to him after I'm finished with the secretary?"

"Good idea."

Ollie put out his hand.

"Welcome aboard."

"Like old times," I said shaking his hand.

"I hope not," he smiled, "I don't know if Vincent could handle it."

"He dragged me in so you know it must be really important."

Ollie smiled.

"This is high profile, at least for this area."

"Speaking of high profile, you talk to Crystal Hudson?"

"No, not yet," he sighed, "she's like a shark."

"No problem. We talked and we made a deal."

He held up his hands like he was pushing me away.

"I don't want to know it."

"The higher ups said this had to be quiet and I stressed that to her."

"She's a reporter, Cameron, she can't be quiet."

"I trust her."

"Good luck."

"Anything else?"

"No, I guess not. Let me know when you talk to Griggs' parole officer. I can hardly wait to see what he says."

"I'll do that," I said.

I left thinking Doreen Tilly might be a bundle of information. I believe bosses tell their secretaries things they wouldn't tell their wives. I didn't believe for one minute Edwin Barnett shared anything with his lovely young wife.

The Barnett Building, huge and glass filled, was south of town. I could work there.

The security guard intercepted us as we walked in.

"ID, please," he said. No smile, all business. I thought he might apply to work for Neda Barnett, but he already worked for the family. These sour expressions I was seeing was beginning to give me the idea that's the type of people they wanted.

I showed him my beautiful picture on my PI card.

"If you need confirmation," I said, "call Oliver Fletcher with SPD."

"No, that's okay."

He looked at Sheila.

"What about her?"

"She's my, uh…"

"Partner," she said. "I'm his partner."

"Do you have an ID?"

"Not yet," she smiled. "I'm just starting out."

"She's in training," I said, "and you know how trainees are sometimes slow to catch on. It may take some time before she gets one."

She stepped on my foot.

He acted like he didn't believe us. Why would he? I wouldn't believe us.

"We're here to see Doreen Tilly," I said.

"I'll call her."

We walked over to the workstation with a large bank of computer screens and keyboards.

"Miss Tilly? This is Walker down in security…two people to see you…man and a woman…private detectives…yes ma'am…bye."

He pointed over my shoulder.

"Take the elevator to the top floor. "You'll step out into The Barnett Company's office lobby."

"Thanks."

The elevator was of the scenic variety. The people and cars got smaller as we rose. I looked down at them until they were the size of ants. Sheila closed her eyes.

"A grand view," I said. "Take a look."

"No thanks."

"You scared of heights?"

"I'm afraid of elevators and heights. I don't need to be riding in one I can see through the walls."

"Suit yourself," I said, "but it is a grand view."

The door opened into a spacious area the size of my apartment. A middle aged slightly overweight woman with dyed black hair sat at a huge desk.

"Miss Tilly?" I asked walking up to her.

"Yes," she said looking up from a book.

She was probably an attractive woman in her younger days, but several things deprived her of that now.

"Lee Cameron," I said putting out my hand. "The guard called about us."

She gave me a stronger handshake than most men.

"This is my assistant, Sheila Arceneaux."

The women nodded to each other but didn't shake hands.

"What can I do for you?"

"Neda Barnett hired me to look into Edwin Barnett's death. You mind if we talk to you?"

"I told that detective all I know."

"Yes, I talked to him, but I'd like to go over it with you again. Maybe you can remember something you didn't at that time."

She closed the book.

"Is that Mr. Barnett's office?" I asked pointing to a large door behind her.

"Yes."

"You mind if we have a look?"

"There's nothing in there right now. They're fixing it up for the new president."

"How about a quick look," I said with my most personable smile.

"I don't know."

"Look, if Neda or Yvonne Barnett say anything tell them I insisted as part of the investigation."

She smiled. "I guess it wouldn't hurt."

We followed her. She was right. The place was torn apart. The desk, chairs, and cabinets were covered with a tarp. The walls were stripped bare. Drop cloths were stuffed into the corners.

"Not much to see," she said.

"I'd like to look at the desk and chair."

"Of course," she said and headed to the door. "I'll be out here when you're finished."

I pulled back the cloth and put it on the floor. I went over the desk. It was covered with dried blood and would be replaced so there wasn't much use in cleaning it. I opened all the drawers. They were empty. I crawled under the desk passing my hand to see if I could feel anything that shouldn't be there. The chair was bloody with a hole in the back. I looked at the back to see a larger hole. I followed the path to see where the cops dug the slug out of the wall.

"Just like Ollie told me," I said.

"Did you expect to find something different?" Sheila asked bending down to the see the hole in the wall.

"No, not really, but I wanted to cast my beady little eyes on the scene."

"Your eyes are not beady. You couldn't be beady if you tried or even knew what it meant."

"I'm always glad I bring you along."

I turned the chair upside down and looked and felt along the legs. I felt something by the knob where you turn the chair to raise and lower it. I looked closer. It was a small strip of black electrical tape about three inches long, the same color as the chair frame. If the person searching wasn't careful or in a hurry, they would miss it. I took out a plastic bag and put the tape in it. I wanted to get it checked for fingerprints. I put everything back like it was.

"What do you think he had taped under there?" Sheila asked.

"Maybe nothing. Maybe something. It might be something he wanted to hide. If so, someone found it, but didn't think it was important enough to remove the tape. Either the killer or someone else."

"Someone else?"

"Like…maybe a secretary."

Sheila smiled. "I knew you were brilliant."

"Let's go," I said.

"You find anything?" Doreen Tilly asked.

"No, but I didn't figure I would."

She held up the book.

"You see how busy I am."

"Who will get this office?"

"I don't know. I'll probably be gone by then."

"Why so?"

"Come," she said, "there's a coffee shop downstairs. We can talk there."

"What about your busy day?" Sheila asked.

"It can wait a while. I'm really not that busy."

The coffee shop was more like a small restaurant. She got her some coffee. I got my usual. Sheila got some disgusting looking health drink.

"What would you like to know?" she said.

"How long did you work for Edwin. Barnett?"

"Thirty years."

"Doing what you do now?"

"Yes. He wasn't always head of the company. When he started out, he was a flunky like everyone else. Yvonne saw to that. She wanted him to learn the business from the ground up, but she also wanted him to have a secretary. I don't know why back then. Anyway, I applied and got hired. I've been here ever since."

"In thirty years, you must have had some interesting conversations with Mr. Barnett."

"Like what?" she asked sweetening her coffee.

"Anything personal?"

"Some."

"Anything you can tell us?"

"I'd rather not. He told me things I know he wouldn't tell his snooty prissy young wife."

"He didn't trust her?" Sheila asked.

"She's a gold digger. I think he saw that after the wedding but didn't want to make a public scene by divorcing her. But I have to say she didn't do anything that embarrassed him publicly."

"What about privately?"

She shook her head and smiled.

"Can't blame me for trying."

"No, I can't.

"What can you tell us about the relationship between Isaac Kruger and Edwin Barnett?"

"Mr. Kruger handled a lot of Mr. Barnett's personal matters."

"Any business dealings?"

"Some, but mostly personal."

"What happened that caused the split?"

"When he decided not to use Mr. Kruger, he told me it was conflict of personalities. I worked for him a long time and I believe there was more than what he was telling me. I did hear them talking pretty loud in Mr. Barnett's office a few days before the split."

"What was it about?" Sheila asked.

"Money. Everything they talked about was about money. Miss Arceneaux, you have to understand something. Mr. Barnett dealt in millions like we deal in ones even in his personal life. The man was richer than any of us could imagine. A million to him was peanuts. I think Mr. Kruger was trying to get him to slow his spending. Taxes and all."

"Didn't he have a CPA to do that?"

"Yes, but Mr. Kruger must have had some interest in it. I don't know."

"You know what Kruger was talking about when you say slow his spending?"

"Not really. One thing could be how much he gave Neda. I can tell you he gave her plenty, but I won't mention amounts. The time I heard them talking so loud, they didn't mention anything in specifics."

"You ever see Mr. Barnett's personal account?"

She smiled again but didn't answer.

I shook my finger at her and smiled.

Sheila pressed on.

"You know of anyone that would want to kill Mr. Barnett? Did he mention any problem with anyone that might lead to his murder?"

"He never said. If he was having some problems that serious, he kept it from me which would be a first."

"Why so?"

"We discussed a lot of his personal feelings, mostly about his wife. I think his will to let her do as she pleased in return for not disrupting his public life bothered him."

"Do you know where she went on her trips?"

"Usually down to Jamaica or one of those islands."

"Was it always out of the country?"

"Always."

"What did Mr. Barnett do when she was gone?"

"Worked late a lot. Spent a lot of time at the club."

"You talking about Hollow Lake?"

"Yes."

She finished her coffee and stood.

"I guess I better get back. I don't have anything to do but read, but Yvonne Barnett wants me to be there just the same. She said it looks professional. And it would look bad if someone came up there and the place was empty. If anything, I can tell whoever does show up what's going on and direct them to the right place, but you're the first ones I've seen since Mr. Barnett died. I mean other than the police."

I stood and shook her hand.

"Thanks, Miss Tilly."

"Doreen, please."

"Doreen."

This time they shook hands.

"Nice to meet you, Doreen," Sheila said.

"Same here."

They both had on their fake smiles.

I handed her a fresh business card.

"Would you please call us if you think of anything?"

"Yes, Mr. Cameron. I will."

"Call me Lee. After all we had coffee together."

"And you can call me Sheila."

We started to go then I thought of something.

"Would you know what happened to his cell phone?"

"No. When I came in that day, I couldn't find it. The police told me the killer probably took it."

"That could be, but I don't know why he would take just that. Was Mr. Barnett accustomed to carrying large sums of cash on him?"

"Yes. I told him I didn't think it was a good idea, but he thought nothing of it."

"It seems strange the killer would take a cell phone, but not check his pockets."

"It certainly does."

"Thanks again," I said.

We stood outside gazing at the glass building. You know the old saying about throwing rocks at glass houses. Someone threw a big rock and it shattered Edwin Barnett.

We walked to my car thinking Doreen Tilly wasn't telling us everything.

"I can see your brain working," Sheila said. "Want to let me in?"

"I feel she's holding something back, but why would she? If she saw his personal accounts, she knew what he was spending his money on."

"I'll bet Yvonne and sweet little Neda didn't know."

"She may be protecting him."

"From what?"

"When I went to see Jack Vincent the other day, he told me Yvonne Barnett didn't want to drag the family name through the mud."

Sheila stopped.

"Maybe Doreen Tilly knows something that would ruin the good Barnett name. Maybe Momma Barnett knows that Doreen knows and is keeping tabs on her…you know keep her around to make sure she, meaning Doreen Tilly, doesn't say something wrong."

"Not even to the police?"

"Not even to the police."

I shook a finger at her, smiling.

"That would be withholding evidence. She could get in big trouble for that."

"Momma Barnett has enough money to buy her out of any trouble."

"Could be," I nodded

"What now?"

"Let's go back to the office and check our mail then we'll head over to Tom's."

When we got to the office, the outside door was open.

"Uh-oh," Sheila said.

"Stay put."

I eased the door the rest of the way and could see my office door still closed. There were no hiding places with all of Sheila's Christmas paraphernalia.

"Maybe he's in your office," she whispered.

I looked at her.

"Why wouldn't it be a she?"

"Just go check."

I turned the knob and slammed it open. If anyone was behind the door, I'd have him…or her. I went inside and looked around. It was empty and it looked like all was in order.

"Look here."

I turned to see her holding an envelope.

"Someone left us a Christmas gift," she said.

There was nothing written on the outside of the envelope.

The message was written in mixed pasted letters, the type you see kidnappers send in the movies. I carefully opened it trying not to smudge any fingerprints. I read it:

Get off the case before someone close *to* you dies

I put it back in the envelope after re-reading it.

"I guess they mean you. You're the only one close to me."

"What are we going to do, Lee?"

It was the first time I heard any anxiety in her voice since she wanted in.

"Well, someone knows I'm on the case so we must have stirred em up. This is their way to try to get me off. It's pretty weak, if you ask me. They obviously don't know me."

I started to put the envelope in my pocket.

"Wait," she said and went to her desk drawer. "Here."

She handed me a gallon zip lock storage bag.

"To preserve evidence," she said.

"Good thinking. I'll make a private eye out of you yet."

I put the envelope in the bag, sealed it and put it in my pocket.

"Let's go to Tom's and discuss it."

"Yeah," she said looking around. "I don't think I want to be in here right now."

We sat at a corner table. I wanted to get as far away from prying ears as I could. So why did we come to such a busy place? Comfort and security are the best way to put it. Sheila felt safe in this crowd. If she feels safe, I'm happy.

"What if whoever did this comes to the office when you're not there? What do I do then?"

"I'm surprised at you, Sheila. After all these years you let one little threat get to you. I thought you were made of tougher stuff."

"No one ever threatened to kill me before."

"If it's any consolation, I'll still find the killer even if he…or she kills you."

"You're all heart."

I patted her hand.

"You want out?"

"I don't think so."

"You don't think? You might want to decide one way or the other. This has the potential to get bad."

She wiped her face with a napkin from the table. She was visibly shaken.

"Everything will be all right. I need to call Ollie about this."

I told Ollie about the note and hung up as Tom came to the table.

"Ollie said he'd get a patrol car around there during our business hours. Does that help?"

"It'll have to," she said.

"What's up?" Tom asked. "You usually sit at the bar."

"Sheila got a letter from her boyfriend and it upset her."

Tom scratched his head.

"You gotta boyfriend? What about Lee?"

I showed him the note.

"Oh," he said. "You rest easy. I'll bring you something to help you relax on the house."

He was gone before we could answer then came back carrying a pitcher and two glasses.

"Drink this," he said, "and I'll guarantee it'll relax you."

"What is it?"

"Don't ask, just drink."

Sheila poured herself a glass and took two big gulps.

"Good. What is it?"

"Something I threw together in the toilet. Enjoy."

He hurried back to the busy bar.

"What's it taste like?" I asked.

"A cross between orange juice and a margarita—"

She took another look drink and smacked her lips.

"—and something else I'd rather not mention."

I poured me a glass and tasted it. Not bad.

It didn't take long to finish the pitcher. Sheila relaxed like Tom said she would, or it could be she was getting sauced.

"Look, Sheila. I know this note shook you up, but I believe it's just a scare tactic. I don't believe there's anything to it. I wouldn't let anything happen to you."

"Oh," she smiled, kind of leaning to the side, "does that mean you still love me?"

"Like a sister. Let's go."

We brought the empty pitcher and glasses to the bar. Tom nodded and waved bye.

"Why don't you take the rest of the day off," I said. "Go home and get some rest."

"No way. I won't let this joker tell me how to run my life. I'm going back to the office."

"But you said—"

"Never mind what I said."

She staggered to her feet, and I helped her out the door.

"Okay, let's go."

On the way back, I wondered if the note writer really meant to try and kill one of us.

6

Friday, December 3rd

Sheila got the name of Philo Griggs' parole officer. She called and set up an appointment for us to see him. His office was just north of what I call the law enforcement center. The jail and parish and federal courthouses are in the area.

The lobby was set up with rows of folding chairs. I saw doors to what could be interview rooms. I didn't believe the workers here would have their offices in public view.

The receptionist/security guard rang Xavier Unger's office. We sat and waited.

"Xavier Unger," the man said entering the lobby.

I expected some burly guy with an attitude. This guy was just the opposite. He was small. His dark suit looked a couple sizes too big and I thought it would swallow him up at any time. His look was topped off with a conservative bow tie.

I stood and put out my hand. His grip was firm.

"Lee Cameron," I said. "This is my associate, Sheila Arceneaux. I think you talked to her on the phone."

"Yes, of course. Nice to meet both of you. Follow me, please."

His office was smaller than I expected, but I guess he didn't need much room just to talk. A small lamp, switched off, was at the edge of the desk centered away from him. A folder occupied one corner. Other than that, his desk was clean. The wall on either side of the room contained photos of our host. Most were of him were of different times in his life with people I didn't know. Some were of him in a karate gi. I also noticed in all of these pictures the belt around his waist was black.

"Mr. Unger," Sheila said, "I see you're into martial arts."

He looked at the pics and nodded.

"In my younger days. Now I teach one night a week at Mr. Yum's Karate Dojo. Mostly to stay in shape and show older people how to protect themselves."

"I guess it comes in handy in your line of work," I said.

Sheila rolled her eyes.

Unger smiled.

"I've never had the occasion to see if it works. Fortunately, for me, I've had cooperative people."

I nodded and shut up.

"Where are my manners?" he said. "Please sit down."

We sat in two wooden chairs in front of his desk. They were not built for comfort.

"Miss Arceneaux said you would like to speak with me about Philo Griggs."

"That's right," I said.

"She said something about a murder."

I looked at the folder on his desk and saw Griggs' name.

"I was hired by Edwin Barnett's wife to investigate the case. She told me Philo Griggs might have a reason to kill her husband. That's why we're here."

He pulled the file in front of him and opened it.

"Mr. Griggs keeps his appointments and stays out of trouble as far as I can tell. He had some bad experiences in prison, and I can assure you he doesn't want to go back. Judging from his actions since he's been out of prison, I would say you have the wrong man. He's been keeping his nose clean, as they say."

"What kind of people does he hang out with?"

"I can't say because I can't keep track of him twenty-four hours a day. He is urged to stay away from the sordid type, if you know what I mean. I also suggested he stay out of bars and clubs and stay away from—"

He looked at Sheila.

"—unsavory women. No offense to you."

"None taken," she smiled. "I would suggest the same thing."

"Of course," he continued, "I can't say if he's following these suggestions, but I haven't gotten any reports of foul deeds."

"Does he have a girlfriend?" Sheila asked.

"Not that I'm aware of."

"Did he tell you why he went to prison," I asked.

"Not much. I knew why. He did tell me what went on there and he doesn't want to go back. He stressed that to me on many occasions. As big as he is, the man is deathly afraid of that place."

"So, he's been a model citizen since his release."

"I believe it's safe to say yes."

"Do you have a picture of Griggs?"

He pulled a photo from the bottom of the stack. The man certainly looked menacing. The picture showed only his head, neck, and shoulders. I could tell he was huge. Unger must have read my mind.

"Mr. Griggs is a rather large man. His weight is more than three hundred pounds, but he is as gentle as a kitten. You might call him a gentle giant."

"You say he had bad experiences in prison," Sheila said.

"Yes, Miss Arceneaux."

"Did he say what?"

"No, but he did say they were not pleasant."

"Did they change his way of thinking?"

"What do you mean?"

"You say he doesn't want to go back to prison. Did he come out with a chip on his shoulder, an attitude toward the establishment?"

"No, I don't think so."

She looked at me.

"I think Miss Arceneaux wants to know what to expect when we talk to him. She doesn't want a bull of a guy to crush us like a grape if we ask the wrong question. I'd like to know the same thing."

He smiled.

"I think it's safe to say Mr. Griggs will cooperate with you. He may look like he's capable of crushing you like a grape, but I don't think he will. He knows that could only mean trouble."

"What does he do for fun?" I asked.

"I believe he prefers to play pocket billiards."

"That would mean going to one of those places you suggested he stay away from," Sheila said.

"Yes, I'm afraid it would."

"The temptation could be there for trouble or unsavory women."

I looked at her. She winked.

Unger didn't notice and went on.

"Yes, it could, but I can't stop him. I can only hope he thinks before he does something that could land him back in jail."

"Do you think he has that capacity?" Sheila asked. "I mean do you think he would think before he acted?"

"I can assure you, Miss Arceneaux; Philo Griggs is not mentally incapacitated in any way. You may see him as a lumbering ox, but his mental faculties are in place. He is not a retard as some like to say."

"Where does he work?" I asked.

"He's a stevedore at the Shelberg port."

"I guess that fits him," Sheila said.

Unger shrugged.

"One might think his size is comparable to the job."

"I think that about covers it, Mr. Unger," I said. "We'll leave you to your work."

"When did you plan on speaking with Mr. Griggs?"

"I guess as soon as we can run him down."

"Would you like me to contact his supervisor? He may be able to help."

"Yes, that would be great."

He turned to the desk phone behind him. No fancy smancy cell phone for this guy.

"Mr. Quint, please…yes, I'll hold."

We sat in silence. I could hear the music coming from his phone.

"Ira? This is Xavier Unger. How is everything? Good. I have a request."

He listened then nodded.

"Yes. Mr. Lee Cameron…yes, the private detective and his associate would like to speak with you about Philo…no, he's not in any trouble…yes, it has something to do with the murder…just a few minutes of your time…wonderful, I'll tell him. Good-bye."

He put the receiver in the cradle.

"Philo Griggs is one of his favorite workers. I believe Ira calls him a real ox, strong as one and indefatigable. He said he would speak with you after lunch. Is that sufficient?"

"Yes," I said.

He looked at Sheila.

"I should tell you Mr. Quint is crude and…how should I say this, full of himself. His language is awful and not the kind of man I would want in the presence of a lady."

I looked at Sheila.

"I'll tell you if I see one."

She punched me on the arm.

Unger saw the humor and laughed a little.

"Thanks for your help," I said shaking his hand.

"I hope this ends in good fortune for Mr. Griggs," he said taking Sheila's hand gently.

She smiled at the attention.

"Mr. Unger," Sheila said.

"Yes, Miss Arceneaux."

"Could you give Mr. Cameron karate lessons?"

He looked at me and smiled.

"I'd be delighted."

I shook my head.

"No, thanks, I'm fine the way I am."

He pulled a small case from this coat pocket, removed a card and handed it to me.

"If you change your mind, call me."

"Don't expect that from me," I said when we were in the car.

"Expect what?"

"The hand thing he did."

"You mean he didn't grab my hand and shake it off my shoulder like some insecure Neanderthal."

"Well—"

"Forget it," she said, "he's cultured and has nice manners, but I prefer a hulking man like you."

"Consider it dropped and what's that about me taking karate lessons?"

She smiled and shrugged.

I let that drop, too.

"We have time before we meet with Ira Quint," I said.

"Pull in there," she said pointing.

There was the parking lot of the main branch of the Greenwood Parish Public Library.

"Okay," I said. "What's on your mind?"

"That note that came today."

"What's bothering you about it?"

"It said someone close to you would be killed if you didn't get off the case."

"Correct."

"You remember what Tom said about the killer?"

"Refresh my memory."

She turned in the seat to face me.

"He said that anyone who could kill someone like Edwin Barnett wouldn't have a problem killing you…or me."

"I won't let anything happen to you."

"You can't be with me every day around the clock."

"You want me to call Ollie and have patrols around your apartment in addition to around the office?"

She shook her head.

"What, then?"

"Maybe I should take the karate lessons."

I smiled.

"Maybe, call Mr. Unger."

I handed her the card.

"Maybe," she said. "Then I could beat you up."

"You can do that now."

"You were always modest."

"It's a gift."

We sat for a while, neither of us saying anything. She studied the card.

"I guess we need to go see Mr. Quint," she said.

I started the car and pulled into the traffic.

"You know you just gave me something else to worry about," I said.

"How so?"

"I don't know if our message today was a bluff, but I have to treat it like it's not. I'll have to keep one eye on you and one on the trail of the killer."

"You do love me," she said smiling.

"Like a sister."

We headed for the Port of Shelberg. If Ira Quint didn't give us any more information than Xavier Unger, I figured the Philo Griggs tree we were barking up was the wrong one.

I stopped at the gate leading into the Port. A burly security guard with a sour face came to the car. He had a full beard which surprised me. I didn't think they were allowed because of safety reasons. The powers that be may have figured he wouldn't need to don a safety mask.

He bent down and looked us over. I showed him my ID and he checked our names off his list. Apparently, Ira Quint let him know we were on the way.

"First building on the right," he said pointing.

"Thanks," I said and drove through.

At first, I thought we were in the wrong place. It looked like a warehouse, a huge empty warehouse. We walked until we came to a small door with SUPERINTENDENT written on the glass.

A full-figured bleached blond receptionist welcomed us.

"We're here to see Mr. Quint," I said.

"Your name, please?"

"Lee Cameron and Sheila Arceneaux."

She lifted a sheet of paper held down on a clipboard and looked at the sheet below it. She looked up at us and back down.

"He's expecting us," Sheila said.

She let the page fall and put the clipboard in a drawer.

"Follow me," she said struggling to her feet. "His office is down the hall."

Ira Quint was what my parents would call a greaser. His hair was slicked back and shiny. He wore a white button-down shirt, that was too tight, unbuttoned to his stomach, blue jeans and loafers with a penny in the slot. For a nice touch he wore white socks. He looked like a throwback to the fifties. He wore a gold chain with a large gold bowling pin so big it stressed the chain.

The receptionist left after she gave him one of those keep your hands off look and glared at Sheila. She obviously had something for Mr. Quint.

His office was decorated with bowling items. Big and small trophies stood as proof as to his ability. Too many pictures crowded both walls on each side of his desk. Most of were of Quint alone holding trophies or just posing. A few were with his bowling team judging from the identical shirts. He obviously liked himself.

"Unger said you wanted to talk to me about Philo Griggs," he said pulling a toothpick from his desk drawer and jamming it into his mouth. His eyes darted between me and Sheila, but he concentrated on her.

"Yes, Mr. Quint—"

"Ira."

"Yes, Ira," I said. "Has Philo Griggs been a problem since he's been here?"

"No, in fact, he's a great worker and don't cause no trouble. Kind of keeps to himself. Any special problem you have in mind?"

"I'm sure you heard about Edwin Barnett's murder."

"Kind of hard not to," he said to Sheila. "A big shot like that gets his ass killed, it's big news and his picture is plastered all over the newspaper and television."

Then he looked at me and sat up.

"You don't think…not Philo….that's ridiculous."

"Mr. Barnett's wife gave us his name. She thinks he might want to do something since Mr. Barnett fired him for theft."

"And dealing drugs on his property," Sheila said.

"I guess when you look at it like that, it's possible," he said relaxing. "Barnett's wife probably has a lot of money and I guess it's easy for her to point a finger at an ex-con who's trying to scratch out a living. How can he fight her?"

"Does he miss much work?" Sheila asked. "Come in late, leave early for no apparent reason?"

He gave her his undivided attention. I wasn't there as far as he was concerned.

"I'll tell you, Miss—"

"Sheila."

"Well, Sheila, Philo never misses no work. He comes in early and leaves late. I guess he don't have much of a life. He never misses or calls in sick. He ain't been here long enough to get vacation time. He's a damn good worker. I need more like him."

"Do you have any other ex-cons working for you?" I asked.

He slowly turned away from Sheila.

"A few. Most are like Griggs. They loners mostly. A few hate the system that sent them up and get riled up now and then."

"Do they get along?"

"For the most part. You have a lot of big men doing heavy tiring work. Tempers get short sometime, but most of the time nothing comes of it."

"Most of the time?"

"We have guys get into it sometimes. No harm done. They kick each other's ass then back to work. All in a day's work."

"Ever call the police on any of those occasions?"

"No, we take care of it. We have a security force. We call the cops and they get put back in the slammer. Most are on parole and they don't need anything to show they went against it. No big deal. Short of somebody getting their ass shot or stabbed, we don't call the cops."

"Philo Griggs ever get short with the others?"

"He's not any different than the others in my eye. Like I said, he keeps to himself, but things happen. He's a big guy. Sometimes the others like to test the big guy, especially if he's new. You know, a man's world."

Then a thought struck him.

"You ain't about to take him away, are you?"

"No, Ira, we're not, but we would like to talk to him."

"Here?"

"If it's not too much trouble."

He rubbed his chin and played with his toothpick.

"I don't like that kind of thing on the job."

"Maybe we could talk to him away from the others. It wouldn't take long."

"He's not here today. One of his day's off."

"I thought you said he never missed work," Sheila said.

This ticked him off.

"Look, he don't miss, but he don't work seven days a week, neither. Don't you get a day off? He don't miss on the days he's scheduled to work. Today's his day off. How's that? Damn."

"Very clear," she said.

She held his eyes until he turned to me.

"He likes to shoot pool. That's what he does most of the time when he's off."

"Does he have a girlfriend?" Sheila asked. I saw her smile.

"I don't know, but he might be banging one of the barflies at the Eight Ball."

"The Eight Ball?"

"The Eight Ball Lounge, but don't let the name fool you. It's nothing but a dive. Mostly the rough ones go there. It can get a little nasty sometimes, but that's normally on the weekends. I don't think a pretty lady like you would want to go to a place like that."

"I can take care of myself."

"I'm sure you can," he smiled.

"Mr. Unger said he suggested Mr. Griggs stay out of those type places."

"Well, darlin, Philo is a healthy man, you know what I mean? And he can go where he wants and do what he wants as far as I'm concerned and as long as he shows up for work."

He moved the toothpick to the other side of his mouth.

"I'm not—" Sheila started.

I figured I needed to jump in and separate them.

"You think he's there now?"

He turned his attention back to me. I don't believe Mr. Ira Quint was accustomed to women talking to him that way.

I caught Sheila's wink at the corner of my eye.

"Probably. He's got a friend he plays with. They're probably together."

"What's his friend's name?"

"Couldn't tell you."

He turned to Sheila.

"It should be pretty calm during the day. A pretty lady like you should be safe."

His smile looked more like a leer.

"I could show you where it's at," he said. "Maybe we can have a drink."

"No thanks," she said, "I don't drink."

"I know where it is," I said.

Sheila looked at me. Her eyes wanted to know how and why I knew where this dump was.

Ira Quint took the toothpick out of his mouth, picked something out of his teeth, and tossed it in the trash can.

"Do you bowl, Sheila?"

"It was never one of my favorite sports."

"I can teach you. I been city champ three years running. Nobody can beat me."

"I bet."

"We better get going," I said standing and put out my hand. "Thanks for your time and the information."

He shook my hand.

"One more thing," I said. "Does Philo Griggs have a short fuse? Miss Arceneaux would like to know that before we talk to him."

"I seen him mad, but I never seen him hit nobody. He keeps it under control pretty much. I don't know if that has somethin to do with his parole, but never seen him in a fist fight, but that don't mean he's never been in one. I'm sure he had plenty in the joint."

"Thanks," I said and headed for the door.

"You come back and see me, Sheila," he said.

Being the nice person she is, she nodded and smiled.

"I'd like to ask you something, Ira," she said.

"Shoot."

"Do you ever go to the Eight Ball and bang the barflies?"

I grabbed her before he could answer and pulled her out.

"What do you think?" I asked her when we were in the car.

"How do you know where that bar is?"

"I know," I said waving to the guard.

"How?"

"I just do. Look you want to go talk to Philo Griggs with me or argue about how I know where the damn bar is?"

She sulked then said, "He makes me want to take a bath."

"You mean Mr. Quint?"

"You know who I mean."

"He certainly doesn't look like the kind of fellow you'd take home to momma."

"I wouldn't take him to a rat hole."

"If you don't like the guy, just say so."

"I don't like him."

"By the way, why did you do that?"

"What?"

"That question about him banging barflies."

"Xavier Unger was right. The man's crude. Okay, where's this bar?"

"Right around the corner."

I headed west away from the port and took the first left off the boulevard. The Eight Ball Lounge was on the left. The parking lot was unpaved. These type of places seldom have paved parking. Why would the owner spend money on paving when his patrons will come anyway? There were two big pickups and a few cars in the lot. The white pickup looked familiar.

I could hear an old country and western song. I was willing to bet it had the old type jukebox with 45s.

"You can sit in the car and wait," I told her.

"Why would I do that?" she said opening her door.

"It could get rough."

"Then I better go. You'll need me. I'm a better fighter than you."

"Are you trying to crush my male ego?"

"No," she said taking a deep breath, "it's just a fact."

I let it drop and closed my door. Our first suspect waited.

The white pickup in question was a dually with two rifles hanging on a gun rack. It had a personalized license plate: SHT2KIL.

"Must be one nice guy," Sheila said.

"What do you think it means?"

"You're kidding."

"It could mean shot to kill or shit to kill," I said smiling.

"It probably means shoot to kill."

She grabbed my arm and led me into the bar. It was like thousands of bars across the country. Cigarette, or some other kind of smoke, and the smell of beer hung in the air.

Sheila scrunched up her nose.

"What do you think the bathrooms smell like?" I asked.

"Not funny and I don't want to find out."

"We may not be here that long."

"You used to come here?" she asked taking in the scenery. "Nice place. I should have known you then."

"Long time ago. It was before I got my bearings straight."

"Your bearings are still not straight. You'll have to tell me about it."

"Some time…maybe."

I was curious about the jukebox, so I went to take a look. I was wrong about the 45s. It was filled with CDs dating back to the old country and western tunes. Somehow, I didn't think one would hear rap or disco or anything else. It reminded me of a line from *The Blues Brothers* when they went to play a country and western gig. The owner of the bar said, "We play both, country and western." I smiled.

"What's so funny?" Sheila asked.

"Flashback to *The Blues Brothers*."

"Never saw it."

"Figures."

I saw two guys shooting pool. One would take a drink from a beer at a booth. They were big and I figured one to be Philo Griggs and his friend Quint told us about. Two "ladies" sat in the booth, one on each side. The term "ladies" could be interchangeable with other terms if you know what I mean.

We went to the bar. The bartender wasn't much bigger than me. I wondered how he could keep order in a joint like this. Then I noticed a gold chain hanging around his neck with a gold pair of boxing gloves attached.

"Can you tell me if Philo Griggs is here?" I asked.

He pointed at the two men.

"The big one."

"They're both big," Sheila said.

He smiled and said, "the biggest one. The one without the cap."

"Thanks," I said.

We sat two booths down from the ladies. Sheila slipped in while I went to make my introduction.

"Philo Griggs?"

The bigger of the two was watching the other set up a shot.

"That's me."

I walked around the table and showed him my ID.

"You mind if we talk to you?"

"We?"

"Me and my associate," I said motioning to Sheila.

He looked at her without much interest.

"What about?"

"Edwin Barnett. You mind?"

He frowned a little then leaned his cue against the wall.

"Be back in a minute," he said to his friend who wore a dirty New Orleans Saints cap.

He watched Philo pick up his beer and squeeze into the opposite side of the booth. I sat next to Sheila. He put out his huge hand to Sheila.

"Philo Griggs. Please to me you."

"Sheila Arceneaux."

He wrapped his hand around the bottle and made it disappear. He took a drink and gently put the bottle down. I caught his friend out of the corner of my eye. He looked interested.

Philo put his hand out to me and I shook it. It was firm, as I expected, but not what I knew he could do to my hand if he took a notion.

"What about Mr. Barnett?" he asked.

"His wife wanted us to check you out," I said. "She thinks you may have killed him."

He shook his head.

"I didn't. Mrs. Barnett, his wife, didn't like me much. Now Mrs. Barnett, his mom, took to me. We got along fine."

"Why didn't Mrs. Barnett, his wife, like you?"

He shrugged.

"I don't know. I never did anything to her. She was good looking and I knew it would be trouble if I even talked to her so I stayed away from her as much as I could."

"Did she ever talk to you?" Sheila asked.

"No."

"Did she ever approach you?"

"No. I think she was scared of me."

"Did she try to do something to get you into trouble with her husband?"

He shrugged.

"I don't know. Mr. Barnett and me got along fine until I messed up everything."

"Why did you steal his stuff," I asked.

"Extra money."

"Didn't you think you'd get caught?"

He shrugged again.

"I guess I didn't think about that at the time. I suppose most thieves don't think about it when it's going on."

"When was the last time you saw Edwin Barnett?" I asked.

"In court when I got sent up."

"Did you threaten him in court that day?"

"No," he said shaking his head. "I said what I said when he ran me off. He didn't press charges until he saw how much I stole. I think at first, he just wanted to get rid of me. It was stupid, but I was pissed, excuse my language."

He sipped his beer.

"I had a good thing with Mr. Barnett. He liked me and I worked hard for him. I made a mistake."

"So, your threat was brought up in court."

"Yeah."

"Do you know who might want to kill Mr. Barnett?" Sheila asked.

He shook his head.

"No, but I can tell you I didn't. I know I may not look too smart, but I'm not that stupid. I don't want to go back to prison. That's no way to live and I'm not doing nothing to go back."

"Hey, Sugar," one the "ladies" called, "you gonna be over there all day?"

"In a minute."

Sheila looked at me. I knew she was thinking about what Ira Quint said about the barflies.

I again caught Philo's friend at the corner of my eye. He was making a feeble attempt at acting like he was playing pool, but I could tell he was listening to what we were saying.

"Look, Mr. Cameron—"

"Lee," I said. "Call me Lee. Mister is too formal."

"Lee. I have a job, maybe not the best in the world, but it's a job. I play a little pool and date some of the ladies. I stay out of trouble. You can ask Mr. Unger, my parole officer, he can tell you."

"We did talk to him," Sheila said, "and he told us the same thing. We also talked to your boss, Ira Quint. He told us you were a good worker. He doesn't want to lose you."

"I hope none of this will get me in trouble. I can't afford to lose my job. It's part of my parole."

I guess Philo's friend couldn't stand it any longer. He came to our booth.

"You playin or not, Philo?"

"In a minute, Hastings. Give me a minute."

Hastings smiled at Sheila and went back to his pretend game of pool.

One of the ladies in the booth went to Hastings, chewed on him a while then went to the bar. She filled up the stool but didn't look that big while she was sitting in the booth.

I took out a card and gave it to Philo.

"Call us if you think of something."

He looked at it then put it in his shirt pocket.

"Be glad to. I know all crooks say they're innocent because they have nothing to lose. I screwed up my life. I know that, but I want to stay on the good side of the law. I wasn't smart enough to play ball in college and I wasn't smart enough to stay out of trouble after that. Maybe it was a good thing Mr. Barnett sent me up. Doing time will change the way you think, at least for some. I saw some that was pissed at the system and wanted to take it out on everybody. I know it changed the way I think about things, and I can tell you, I didn't kill Mr. Barnett. I was mad cuz he let me go, but not that mad."

"Nice little speech," Hastings said. We hadn't noticed he was back.

"I gotta go," Philo said.

He shook our hands, picked up his bottle, and went back to his game.

I rubbed my neck on the way to the door. I turned to see Hastings whatever his name was watching us.

"Hold it a minute," I said.

"Where are you going?"

"Get rid of an itch."

I walked up to Hastings and put out my hand.

"Lee Cameron."

"Hastings Ramby."

He squeezed my hand until I winced. That pleased him. I was glad to feed his ego.

"Do I know you?" I asked rubbing my hand.

"Never seen you before."

He bent over the table to break.

"That your truck out there?" I asked getting past my bruised hand and ego.

"Which un?"

"The one that says, 'shit to kill'."

"That's 'shoot to kill'."

He fired the cue ball at the rack and scattered the balls, but not sinking any.

"You hunt?"

"Yeah. Deer."

He stepped closer and I believe it surprised him when I didn't back up.

"And I don't miss."

"Thanks. Hastings, isn't it?"

"Yeah, that's it."

I went back to Sheila but could still feel his eyes on me.

"Did you get rid of your itch?"

"I don't know. He looks familiar, but I just can't place him."

"What do you think?" I asked when we were back in the car.

"I think we need to go to my apartment."

"Oh," I smiled. "Is that an invitation?"

She ignored my question.

"It's five o'clock. We can pick up some greasy fast food and gorge ourselves."

"How can I turn down an invitation like that?"

She put her hand on my leg. When I looked at it, she took it off.

"This private eye stuff is tiring," she said laying her head back and closed her eyes.

"You haven't done anything, yet. We're just getting started."

She didn't answer.

"Thinking about giving it up already?"

She opened her eyes, looked at me, said nothing then closed them.

I shut up and drove.

We left the Eight Ball Lounge and headed for The 10th Inning. I called Ollie and told him what we found out. He didn't have anything new to report. I told him I would be out of pocket for the weekend.

"Good luck," he said.

I told him I probably would have some kind of luck and hung up.

The afternoon and evening crowds were changing places. There was little change in the mass of bodies while one group left and the other entered. We squirmed our way to the bar. I couldn't tell you how many soft body parts I touched while pushing through the crowd. We claimed two stools at the bar. Tom was bouncing around like a pinball. He did find time enough to give us a wave.

"Well," I said to Sheila, "how was your first day on the job?"

"I don't know if you could call it my first day. I do your phone work for you and other little things that secretaries are supposed to do while avoiding the good stuff."

I held my hand up.

"Let me re-phrase that. How was your first day of rubber hose interrogation?"

Each of Tom's televisions had a different game on, but no sound. We wouldn't be able to hear it anyway."

Sheila looked around the room. All we could see were heads.

"Can't we go somewhere quieter?"

"Such as?"

Tom finally made his way to us. He was breathing hard. The ever-present towel rested on his shoulder."

"Busy day," he said and commenced to wipe the bar. "What'll you have?"

"Just something to go," I said. "Sheila wants me over at her place."

He looked at her and smiled.

"It's about damn time."

"He's wishing," she said. "I invited him over to discuss the case."

"Okay. Sure. What would you like?"

"A couple of your best sandwiches."

"Coming right up."

"You are wishing," she said after he left.

Sheila watched the people. I watched the games. Neither was interesting.

"That was a nasty crack," I said, "about Tom's food being greasy. I'll give you a break and not tell him."

"On the house," Tom said when returned holding two bags.

He spread his arms.

"Are you sure you want to tear yourself away from all this?"

"I'm sure," Sheila said.

"You're bound to see someone here who likes Lee."

She pretended to search the area.

"I don't think so."

"Come on," I said. "I've had as much humor as I can stand."

He smiled at us and headed back into the war zone.

Tom was smart to build his place next to the spacious Greenwood Mall. There was a steady stream of cars in and out, especially this time of year.

I pulled out and hung a left on Shelberg Drive heading north. Sheila lived at the Sawwood Apartment Complex close to the city park. Her place was better than mine. A friend of mine once told me women are nest builders. That's why their place is always more homey than a man's. That's probably one of the reasons why I would rather stay at her place.

As usual, there was no parking space close to her apartment. She liked living on the second floor, so we made our way up. She let us in. I put our bags on the table.

"I found it interesting," she said taking two beers from her refrigerator.

"What? Me?"

"You're always interesting," she said, "in some sort of little kid way."

"I can always depend on you to prop up my ego."

She walked out onto her small balcony. I suppose it would be called a patio if it was on the ground floor. I grabbed the bags and followed like the little pup I was.

Some kids below us ran and screamed at whatever kids do when they were unattended. Dusk was sneaking up on us.

"Oh, this is good," she said taking a bite from her sub. "Tom makes the best sandwiches."

"Not bad for free."

"It would be good if you paid double."

"Maybe you need to talk to him about making commercials."

Sheila put her sandwich down on a napkin, wiped her mouth then took a long pull on the beer.

"That's what I like about you," I said, "all lady."

"I don't have to be a lady here."

"I'll keep that in mind."

"What would your doctor say if he saw you? Beer and semi-fast food. He'd be proud of you, I'm sure."

"He would probably want one, too."

"Did we get any useful information on our witch hunt?"

I put my sandwich and beer on the table. I wiped my mouth with my pinky in the air to show my good manners.

"I don't think Doreen Tilly is telling us everything she knows. She's playing dumb probably waiting to see what the cops will come up with. What does your woman's intuition tell you about her?"

She shrugged and took another bite.

One of the kids screamed. I got up and went to the edge against the railing to see what was going on.

"It's nothing," she said. "It goes on all the time."

I returned to my seat and my beer.

"I don't know," she said. "I'm not used to this interrogation—"

"For safety's sake," I interrupted, "let's call it questioning. Interrogation is something the police do.

"Okay. I'm not used to this type of questioning. I don't know the protocol."

"The protocol is you ask the question. If you don't get the answer you want, you pull out the rubber hose."

"She didn't seem nervous. She would be if she was hiding something, wouldn't she?"

"Not necessarily. It would depend on how much practice she gets. I'm willing to bet she's covered for Barnett on many occasions. Especially if he wanted to keep something from Neda and I'd bet he did that a lot."

"You mean lie for him?"

"I prefer cover. You ever cover for me?"

She finished her sandwich and smiled.

"No, but I lied on occasion."

We heard another voice down in the yard. It must have been the mother of the imps rounding them up for the night. It got quiet when they were inside.

"What about Unger and Quint?" I asked.

"What about them?"

"Do you think they have anything to hide?"

"I doubt it. Why would they?"

"They shouldn't. Quint's boss probably told him no trouble from any of the ex-cons."

I finished my beer and wrapped it in the paper.

"We don't know if he was blowing smoke or not."

"You think he would get fired if Philo Griggs acted up?"

"Quint?"

She nodded.

"Possible, but Unger is just doing his job. I think they're both telling us the truth. Unger doesn't have total control over Philo Griggs."

She sat quiet for a while then looked at me.

"Maybe I should take those lessons."

I looked at her. She was sipping her beer.

"I was only kidding about that."

"Don't you want me safe and sound?"

"Absolutely, but I don't want you to get beat up by people who don't know you even if it would be considered training."

"I'll think I'll take it. Both of us could take them."

"I'll pass."

She sipped her beer and smiled. I hate it when she does that.

"Now, that brings us to the star of the show up to now, Philo Griggs."

"My woman's intuition tells me he didn't do it."

"Do you think he was honest? He tried to put on a good show if he isn't."

"He told us the same thing Mr. Unger told us. He doesn't want to go back to prison."

"I've never heard of an ex-con who did."

It was dark by this time and we moved inside.

"What about his buddy?" Sheila asked.

I shook my head.

"I've seen that guy before. And that truck. It's all familiar, but I can't seem to place them."

She put her arms around my neck. We touched noses.

"This is not good for work relations," I said. "What would your boss say?"

"I won't tell him if you won't."

"Deal."

She pulled away.

"I'm going take a shower and slip into something…well, you figure it out."

"I'll work on it."

I went back to the balcony and looked out into the darkness. From where her apartment was, the only lights were those from the different apartments surrounding the large play area.

I thought Neda Barnett was making me chase wild geese, but she was paying the big bucks, so I chased them.

I took my turn in the shower when Sheila finished. We lay in bed in our birthday suits.

"Do I get a raise for this?" she said.

"I'll talk to the boss, but he can be stubborn when it comes to his money."

"I know how much money he has. He can afford it."

An hour later we were still in bed, but a little tired.

"Lee," she said.

"Don't tell me how wonderful I was."

"I wasn't."

"I'll let that slide."

She reached over and turned on the lamp.

"Take a good look at these."

"I've seen—"

"Not those," she said holding out her forearms. "These. Take a good look."

I had the sinking feeling that our period of intimacy was done.

The scars ran from her wrists for about six inches. They were wide.

"What's this all about?"

"You want to know about these don't you?"

"I'll admit I'm curious, but it's your business. Your past. I prefer our future."

"I want to tell you."

"Look, Sheila. You have your reasons for not telling me or anyone else what happened. I can live with that."

"But you'll always wonder."

"I guess so, but—"

"No but."

She sat up against the headboard and pulled the sheet up to her shoulders.

"This happened about ten years ago. We were married less than a year. Like a lot of women, I thought I found the perfect guy. Physically he was. Blond hair, blue eyes, muscular. He looked great in bikini trunks. We met on the beach. I was laying there. He kept walking by. Back and forth, back and forth. I don't know how many times until he stopped, and we talked.

"We talked for a while. It was about nothing. The weather, the beach. It was like he was trying to work up the nerve to ask me out. Eventually he did. He was nice while we dated. Then one day he asked me to marry him."

She slapped herself on the forehead.

"I didn't, or wouldn't, see what he really was. All I could see was those eyes and that body."

I looked down at mine. It definitely wasn't the surfer type like her Mr. Wonderful back then.

"It wasn't all that great," she said when she saw what I was doing. "In fact, it was bad. The body and looks were tools to get what he wanted. The sex wasn't worth a jerk."

She smiled and covered her mouth.

"Anyway, we got married."

"What kind of work did this man do?"

"He worked in his father's bank if you want to call it work. I really don't know what he did, but it wasn't work. I don't think he got along with his father because his mother would come to our apartment to talk to him. He always made me leave the room, but they talked so loud, I could have stayed with them. She was always trying to smooth things over between them.

"That's when I found out about his temper. He hid it from me the whole time we dated. I didn't think anyone could do that, but he did."

She stopped and wiped her eyes.

"Sheila, you—"

She put up her hand and shook her head.

"Our sex life deteriorated. As bad as it was, it was better than nothing. Obviously not for him. Then he started to come home late. And, of course, he was drunk…and mean. Then one night he came home with…"

She stared straight ahead. If I could see inside her head, I probably would see her replaying whatever it was she was trying to tell me.

I scooted closer to her and kissed her salty cheek.

She wiped her face with a tissue from the nightstand.

"He…he came home with another woman. He said she was an old friend from school and needed a place to stay. I told him no. He said she will. We got in a big shouting match."

She looked at me.

"You want to know the strange thing about this?"

I shrugged.

"Only if you want to tell me. You tell me only what you want."

"I'll tell you. She started undressing. I couldn't believe it. Here we were fighting and she was stripping. I mean down to nothing then she stood there butt ass naked while we shouted at each other."

Then she started laughing one of those hysterical laughs.

"If…if…it wouldn't…have been so…sad, it would have been funny."

She shut up. Not one word for a few minutes. I didn't know if I should say something or not. I was afraid if I said the wrong thing, it might set her off.

"I need a beer," she said.

"Me too," I said jumping out of bed.

I opened it and handed it to her. She took a long pull and I thought she would suck the whole thing down.

"This should be a sad story," she said wiping her mouth, "and I guess it is in a way, but it's not making me sad like I thought it would. Oh, I'll cry, but I wanted to tell someone."

She looked at me.

"Thanks, Lee."

"For what?"

"For not interrupting or criticizing me. He did that a lot."

I kissed her on the cheek again. And waited.

"Anyway, this woman who I didn't know was standing naked in front of us. She crawled in bed, my bed, and said 'will this take long'?

"I stopped and turned on her. I called her every name I could think of. He slapped me. He was defending her.

"Then he started undressing and told me to go wait in the kitchen. He said it wouldn't take long. I knew from experience it wouldn't."

I covered a laugh.

"You can laugh if you want."

"Sheila—"

"No, it's okay."

She started laughing, too. Then we were both hysterical. We spilled our beers but didn't care.

She turned the switch back to serious.

"I did like he told me. I'd decided it was over. I mean, when your husband brings home another woman and crawls in bed with her in front of you that would pretty much means it's over.

"I cried a river while sitting at the kitchen table. I could hear them in the bedroom making all those noises over nothing. So, I went to a drawer and took out the biggest knife I could find and sat back at the table.

"I had a major dilemma and was trying to figure out how to handle it. Should I kill him? Should I kill her? Should I kill both of them? Should I kill myself?"

She didn't answer her own question right off.

I waited.

"I chose to kill him," she finally said.

Uh-oh. Did she?

"I stood up gripping the knife as tight as I could and went in the bedroom. They were tangled up in the sheets making some barbaric noises. It sounded like they were trying to kill each other.

"Then Miss Naked Body saw me, her being on the bottom. She yelled that I had a knife, but I could only stand there with it over my head ready to plunge it into him. I couldn't do it."

She looked at her forearms.

"Well, he jumped up and out of bed before I knew it. He grabbed my arm with the knife and twisted it. I let it fall. He knocked me against the bathroom door, and I fell sitting down.

"Then he…he…"

Silence again. And I waited again sipping my beer. I don't know how it got there, but hers was on the nightstand.

"Then he walked over to me. I could feel blood in my mouth and on my chin. He squatted down with the knife.

"'You know what I think?' he said. 'I think you really want to kill yourself.' He held the knife up and grabbed one of my arms turning it where the inside part of my forearm was up. 'I'll help you,' he said.

"Then he stuck the knife in my wrist and dragged it up. He did the same with the other arm. Blood was everywhere. Miss Naked Body screamed, grabbed her clothes, and left running and yelling that we were both crazy.

"Maybe we were. I looked down at my arms. They were red. I wanted to die at that moment."

She was sitting straight up. The sheet had fallen from her shoulders.

"I really did," she said looking at the far wall, but I knew it wasn't the wall she was looking at.

"Then he did something I never thought would happen. He called 911. He told them I tried to kill myself and needed an ambulance. Then he put the knife in my hand and squeezed it shut. I guess he wanted my fingerprints on it. Then he left and I never saw him again."

She leaned back against the headboard and finished her beer.

"They showed up and took me to the hospital. Of course, I had to go through some therapy because I tried to commit suicide."

"Didn't you tell them what happened?"

"Yes, I did, but they didn't believe me. They said I was hysterical that I wasn't thinking straight. They said a rich kid like him wouldn't do something stupid like that.

"I found out later his dad was a big contributor to the hospital. As far as they were concerned, I was a suicide case and would need treatment. You know something else?"

"There's more? I don't know if I can take more."

She patted my cheek.

"You're sweet, but I'm almost finished."

"Go on."

"I went through therapy to cure my urge to kill myself. I don't remember how long it took or what I had to do, but one day I was cured. They told me I could go. That was that."

"The end?"

"Except for one more thing."

I was afraid to ask but did.

"What?"

"Do you know what all this cost me? The hospital stay, the surgeries on my arms, the therapy."

"No."

"I don't either, but I never received a bill from the doctor or the hospital or from that place where I took my therapy. I didn't have any insurance and I certainly didn't have any money."

"You think he paid it?"

"No, but I think his mom bailed him out and paid everything to keep it quiet. I don't think it was his dad. They didn't get along. I think dear old dad would have let him crash and burn."

She looked at me.

"Now you know what happened."

"Does this guy have a name?"

"Yes."

"What is it?"

"I don't know if I should tell you."

"Why?"

"You might know him."

"That didn't happen around here. How would I know him?"

"You know lots of them."

"Come on. Are going to tell me his name?"

She started laughing.

"His name is…asshole."

"What?"

She nodded then we both broke down. More beer on the sheet. We still didn't care.

"Look at this bed?" she said. "We can't sleep in this. We'll smell like a brewery."

I went to her side of the bed and pulled the sheet back.

"What are you doing?"

I lifted her and carried her into the living room. I put her on the sofa.

"We can sleep, or whatever, in here."

She grabbed me around the neck and pulled me down.

"Do you think any different of me now?"

"No way," I said and kissed her.

"Now, it's your turn," Sheila said.

We were lying on the sofa in the dark. I looked at my watch. It was three am.

"My turn for what?"

"The Eight Ball. Why did you know about it?"

"Oh, that."

"Yes, that. I told you my story. You tell me yours."

"I already told you the one about my short career in law enforcement."

She snuggled closer to me. I enjoyed the warmth of her body.

"I want another one," she said.

"Where to begin," I said.

"At the beginning."

"I was 18 at the time, I think. My buddy had a friend who ran the Eight Ball, and he went there a lot to play pool. One day he told me to go with him. I told him I was only 18."

"A mere child," she remarked.

"Yes, at some things then."

"Really?"

"Yes, really, but that's another story."

"Let's get through this one."

"Well, he told me my age didn't matter so I went with him."

"Lawbreaker," she muttered. I know she was smiling.

"Anyway, I went with him. The place then wasn't any different than it is now."

"Barflies?"

"All those type of places have barflies."

"You seem to know about those things."

"Do you want to hear this story?"

"I do. I do."

"My buddy's friend waved at us when we walked in. He didn't check my ID or anything., but I felt uncomfortable. I was definitely the youngest person there. It wasn't very busy. A couple of guys were playing pool, my buddy got us a couple of beers."

"Does your buddy have a name?"

"Yes, everyone has a name and it's not asshole."

"What is it?"

"Buddy."

"Your buddy's name is Buddy?"

"Yes."

"Continue."

"The place had three pool tables back then. And it was on that day it became a one table bar."

"Did little Lee spill his beer on the felt?"

"Not me."

"Continue."

"Buddy and I decided to shoot a game. The pair next to us had an abundance of beer bottles at the booth. They would drink between shots. I must say they weren't very good because they took a lot of drinks. And they were kind of wobbling."

"This doesn't end well, does it?"

"Not for some people present that day."

"Continue."

"We were into our game, you know, minding our own business when one of the guys staggered over and bumped me while I was lining up a shot. He told me to watch out. I reminded him, in my gentlemanly manner, that he bumped me. His friend pulled him back to the table and they finished their beers. The second guy was walking around the table, and I could see he wasn't any steadier than his friend."

"Is that a word?" Sheila said. I thought she had fallen asleep.

"Is what a word?"

"Steadier."

"It is for this story."

"It's your lie. Tell it like you want."

"It's all the gospel truth."

"Continue."

"He bumped our table and when he went to catch himself, he slipped and messed up our balls."

"What were your balls doing on the table."

"Very funny."

I had to wait for her to quit laughing and snorting.

"Continue," she said when she finally settled down.

"I happened to look over at Buddy who was looking at his friend behind the bar who was shaking his head. I didn't tell you Buddy had a bad temper and he was full of those guys. Well, Buddy started to the first guy, who was by this time lying face down across our table trying to push himself upright."

"Don't," his friend behind the bar said.

"But Buddy didn't listen. By that time the second guy was looking at Buddy, but Buddy was heading toward the first guy. I was looking at the second guy. The bartender was looking at all of us."

"I bet you can't repeat that," she said.

"Repeat what?"

"Who was all looking at who."

"I won't even try."

"Then what happened?"

"Aren't you supposed to say 'continue'?"

"Continue."

"Buddy grabbed the first guy and threw him across their table. The second guy came around their table with a cue stick in his hand. The bartender came out from behind the bar."

"And where were you?'

"Off to the side watching."

"The brave one?"

"I was only 18."

"Continue."

"The second guy swung the stick and hit Buddy up beside the head. The stick broke in two. Well, Buddy didn't flinch and—"

"Wait a minute," she said putting her hand up to my face.

"What?"

"He didn't flinch? It didn't knock him down?"

"No."

"Is this a true story?'

I held up my hand in the dark.

"Scout's honor."

"Continue."

"Buddy grabbed the end in the second guy's hand and pulled him forward. The guy is too drunk, or dumb, to let go so when he was in range, Buddy hit him in the jaw. The guy fell back into the bartender and both of them fell on the floor."

"So, you had one guy laying across a pool table and two more on the floor."

"Correct."

"Was Buddy's head bleeding."

"Yes."

"Did he go to the hospital?"

"No, but he went behind the bar and cleaned his head and threw the bloody rag in the trash."

"So, what happened to the pool table to make them get rid of it?"

"Nothing."

"Nothing?"

"Nothing."

"Then why did he get rid of it?"

"They just wanted one."

"So, getting rid of the pool table had nothing to do with the fight?"

"Nothing."

Sheila took a deep breath.

"It's not a true story, is it?'

I held up my hand in the dark.

"It is. Scout's honor."

"I don't believe you ever in the Scouts. Let's go to sleep."

She snuggled closer, if that was possible, and I snuggled closer to her.

"Lee," she said.

"Yes?"

"What happened to Buddy?"

"What do you mean what happened to him?"

"Did ya'll remain friends?"

"Yes, but we lost touch after a while. I don't have any idea where he is now or if he's still alive."

"You need to contact him."

"Why?"
"You were friends. Friends need to stay in touch."
"Okay, I will."
"Now can we get some sleep?"
And we did.
But I never did try to contact Buddy.

7

Monday, December 6th

The rest of the weekend wasn't as intriguing as the Friday night. We went to the mall Saturday. Sheila wanted to get out and window shop. I thought window shopping was just looking at stuff. She bought more stuff to decorate her office. I really didn't know where she would put it. Sunday, we lazed around her apartment. I brought her to pick up her car Sunday afternoon and spent the night at my place.

Sheila left my apartment early and was at the office by the time I got there. All of her new decorations were up and the maze turned into an obstacle course to get through her office.

"Merry Christmas," she smiled.

I looked at the calendar.

"It's still 19 days away."

She got up and hugged me then pecked me on the cheek.

"I had a wonderful weekend. I feel so much better and it's because of you."

I felt my face warm.

"You're blushing."

"Yeah. You do that to me."

She sat back down.

"I think I'll stay in today. I need to catch up on some work here and uh…Lee…"

Oh, boy, what was coming next?

"Yes."

"I think I'll take some time off from the PI stuff. Do you think you can handle it alone?"

I shook my head.

"I don't know, but I'll try. It was rough going, but you smoothed the way."

"Enough. What's going on today?"

"I need to go see Ollie. Would you call him and tell him I'm on my way? See if you can set up an appointment for me to see Isaac Kruger and see if you can get hold of Yvonne Barnett. I want to talk to her."

"Something missing with her?"

"According to Jack Vincent, she laid down the law to them. I want to see what the law is. Maybe she can give me some inside information."

The sky was clear, but the temperature had dropped to the mid-fifties. I bundled my fragile body against the cold and set off. At least, it was cold to me.

The receptionist let me walk back to Ollie's office alone. I guess they're beginning to trust me.

"Come in, Cameron," he said putting out his hand. "I hope you had an enjoyable weekend while we worked to protect you."

I shook his hand and sat down.

"It was interesting to say the least."

"What do you have?"

"I know I told you we talked to Griggs' parole officer and boss and to Griggs himself. Anything you need to know or share with me?"

"What was Griggs' attitude?"

"He acted like he wanted to help us. Unger, his parole officer, told us Griggs had some bad experiences in prison—"

"I'll bet," he said.

"And he doesn't want to go back. Griggs backed up his story. For a man his size, he appears really afraid of going back."

"I guess size doesn't matter when you're out numbered."

"Anyway, he told me he'd help as much as possible. The funny thing is I believe him."

"Is that your gut feeling?"

"It was the feeling I got when Neda Barnett gave me his name. I knew he could have a motive, but my gut feeling was he didn't do it and after talking to him, I have my doubts about his guilt."

Then I remembered something.

"Can you check on Hastings Ramby?"

"Who's he?"

"He's one of Griggs' friends. They were playing pool when we talked to Griggs. Ramby looked mighty interested in about what we were talking about. I'm just curious if you have anything on him."

Ollie picked up the phone and made a call.

"I'll let you know when I hear something."

"You have anything I should know about?"

"No. We're doing the standard investigation."

"Is everything quiet?"

He nodded and tapped a folder on his desk.

"Yeah. Yvonne Barnett checks in on occasion to see how things are going. I always have this folder on my desk in case she shows up."

"She doesn't talk to Jack?"

"No, she talks to me since I'm heading up the investigation."

"Looks like we have a new chief," I said smiling.

"You talk to her?"

"No, but I will. Sheila is trying to set up a time for me to meet her. And I'm going talk to Isaac Kruger if I get an appointment with him."

"Suppose he won't talk to you? I understand he's not a big fan of Edwin Barnett at this time dead or alive."

"I'll run him down. He will talk to me, or I'll know the reason why."

"Be careful with him, Cameron. He can cause as much trouble for you as Yvonne Barnett. And then it will be all over the papers. Crystal Hudson will have a field day."

His phone rang.

"Yes…he'll be glad to hear that…okay, I'll tell him…bye. That was Sheila. She said Isaac Kruger will meet you at the club. She said he'll be there most of the morning so you can go when you're ready. He's probably talking about Hollow Lake."

"Golf and tennis. Not my sports."

"You know a tie and coat are required to get in. You're not exactly dressed for an upper crust social function."

"This is not a function. I'll get in like I am. Nobody will die if they see me out of uniform."

He stood and said, "Good luck."

"You want to come?"

"No thanks. I have things to do around here. Let me know what you find out or if I need to bail you out."

Hollow Lake Golf and Tennis Club is south of town in an isolated area. Hollow Lake subdivision, a gated community, is across the street.

I parked in the general parking lot as opposed to the reserved lot. The general lot wasn't covered.

I walked in and was met by a staunch old man dressed in a suit standing at a podium. I thought he might be ready to give a speech.

"I'm here to see Mr. Kruger."

He looked me over.

"A coat and tie are required," he said.

"Mr. Kruger is expecting me."

He picked up a phone and turned around. I'm sure he was telling Isaac Kruger that some ruffian was here to see him.

"Mr. Kruger will be right out."

"Thank you."

I walked around watching members, I assumed, come and go. They looked at me like my old friend there looked at me. He watched my every move. I guess he was afraid I would make off with one of the valuables.

"Mr. Cameron."

I turned to see Isaac Kruger. It was the first time I had met the man face to face. He stood at least six and half feet and broad. He had a tough looking face that would scare a bulldog. I saw he was dressed casual.

"Mr. Kruger."

We shook hands.

"Mr. Kruger," said the old man, "the rules state—"

Kruger held up his hand.

"I'll take care of it. Mr. Cameron and I need to discuss something very important. We'll be in the lounge."

"Yes sir," he said, but I could feel his eyes on me.

Kruger led me to a darkened room. This was the lounge. It was bigger than my apartment. We sat on each side of a booth.

"What will you have?" he asked.

"Coke will be fine."

He smiled and motioned a waiter over.

"My usual and a coke for my guest."

The waiter looked at me, shrugged then left.

"Thank you for seeing me on such short notice," I said.

"My pleasure. I'm taking a day off and when I do I like to spend it here."

"I don't have Leprosy or anything contagious like they were looking at me. I didn't want to give them a stroke."

He smiled.

"Think nothing of it. You see this?"

He motioned to his clothes.

"I dress like this all the time unless we have something formal going on. It drives them nuts. Some of the old timers, like Frank up front, are sticklers for the rules."

"But you can get away with it."

"Yes, because I dump a lot of money in this club, so they tolerate me. They don't like what I do, but they put up with it because of the money. That's what it comes down to."

The waiter brought our drinks.

"Okay, Mr. Cameron, let's get on with it."

I sipped my coke and wondered what it cost here.

"First, I want to tell you I'm working independently, but reporting to Detective Oliver Fletcher with the Shelberg Police Department. I was brought on board by Jack Vincent, Melody Broussard and Ursula Daniels. They gave me their blessing."

"Ursula. What an arrogant bitch. She thinks she's a good lawyer. If she was, she wouldn't be on the government payroll. She'd be in private practice where the real money is."

It was obvious what his primary concern was.

I took another sip of coke and put in on the napkin.

"Before all that happened, Neda Barnett hired me to find Edwin Barnett's killer."

"Oh, yes, young Neda. I never could see what Edwin saw in her other than she was quite younger than him and had a nice body, but her attitude is that she married money and could do whatever she wanted. I suppose she's right since Edwin didn't do anything to curtail her activities. And he gave her a lot of money and never asked why. He just handed it over."

Kruger finished his drink and held up his hand. The waiter was there. He must have been waiting. He left and returned with our refills.

"I don't how to say this, Mr. Kruger, so I'll just say it. Neda Barnett gave me your name as a possible suspect."

He grunted and smiled.

"She thinks I would kill Edwin?"

I leaned forward.

"Mr. Kruger, I don't think you killed Barnett—"

"Mr. Barnett. He deserves that much respect."

"Mr. Barnett, but I need to run down the leads."

"Aren't you going to ask me if I killed him?"

"Did you?"

"No."

"Do you have an alibi?"

"What day was that?"

"The coroner put his death at November seventeenth, about one week before Thanksgiving at about ten that night."

He tapped his finger on the table and sipped his second drink.

"No, Mr. Cameron, I don't have an alibi. Does that make me guilty?"

"It makes you a good suspect for the cops."

"Look, Edwin and I were friends for a long time. We had a falling out and I was pissed. I still don't know why he yanked the account from me."

"You think he was hiding something."

"When I was doing his legal work, he kept his nose clean. After he pulled it, I wouldn't know."

"I'll assume Neda Barnett was just throwing names out when I asked her."

"Fine with me."

"Would she have any reason to kill him?"

"Why would she? He gave her everything she wanted. You know she took these trips out of the country once a month."

"Yes."

"He never questioned where she went or who she went with."

"Do you think she had a guy on the side, a young guy?"

He shrugged and finished his drink. Up went the hand. Mine was still half full, but that didn't matter. The table was filling up with glasses.

"Do you know who might want to kill him?" I asked.

"No."

"Do you know Philo Griggs?"

"Yeah, the ex-con."

"Do you think he would kill him?"

"Edwin caught him stealing. He would at least have a motive."

"And you don't?"

"Mr. Cameron, do you know who I really am?"

"A very prominent attorney."

"Is that all you know about me?"

"Sorry, yes."

He motioned for the waiter.

"Go get Frank, please."

The old man came to the booth.

"You need to see me, Mr. Kruger?"

"Yes, Frank. Please tell this gentleman who I am."

Frank looked at me and straightened his tie.

"Mr. Isaac Kruger is the founder and owner of the area's largest and most prestigious law firm in the area. He represents some of the most prominent people in Shelberg and the surrounding area. He donates many millions of dollars to Hollow Lake Golf and Tennis Club. He contributes as much to various charities. He is on the board of most of the charities he donates to. He is past president of the club and its most prominent member. And last, but not least, his success rate in court is ninety-nine percent."

"Thank you, Frank."

Frank bowed like the good servant he was and left.

"Only ninety-nine percent?"

"Can't win em all," he smiled, "but I try."

I finished my second coke.

"Mr. Kruger, I appreciate you talking to me, and I appreciate your patience."

"Not at all. It will be interesting to find out who killed Edwin. And why."

"I'll do my best."

He walked me to the door.

"Good luck, Mr. Cameron," he said putting out his hand.

"Oh, you mind if I ask you one more thing?"

"Shoot."

"Did Yvonne Barnett get along with her son?"

"As far as I knew. If they didn't get along, they didn't show it front of me, but I'll tell you one thing I do know. Edwin did whatever Yvonne wanted. He caved into her wishes, or if you will, her orders. She ran him and she ran the company."

"But she couldn't keep him from marrying Neda."

"That is the only thing she couldn't do with him."

"Thanks," I said and left the sanctity of the club.

8

Friday, December 10th

The end of the week. Sheila's getting antsy with Christmas closing in. She watched the crowds from my office window. She talked me into going shopping with her during the week. She just can't enough of this time of year and continues to buy decorations. She didn't buy much this time; I didn't buy anything.

We're both pretty much alone in the world. That might be another reason we're together. At least we have each other…and of course, our health.

I got to the office early this morning to take care of some business: paid the utilities, the rent, insurance. I also made a list of miscellaneous items Sheila swore we needed. Most were of the Christmas variety.

I left my office door open so I could hear the outer door open while I partook of my liquid breakfast.

I was looking through the newspaper when I heard the door open.

"That you, Sheila?"

No answer.

I waited. She'd come busting in at any time.

But no one did.

"Come on, Sheila," I called, but there was still no answer.

I got up and went to her office. The door had a small crack, but no one was there. Acting the juvenile, I tiptoed to the door. Then it burst open and surprised the crap out of me.

"Good morning," she said carrying in some packages.

I was back against her desk.

"What's the matter?" she asked moving me aside and dumping her loot on her desk. "You look like you saw a ghost."

"Did you open that door?"

"Yes."

"I mean earlier."

"Yes. I forgot something and went back to the car."

She stopped and looked at me.

"Did the big bad man get scared?"

"I heard the door and when you didn't come in, I got up to check. That's when you opened the door on me. I was surprised, not scared."

"Right," she smiled.

"What do you have there?"

"Things."

Uh-oh. This didn't sound good. If she had something in there for me, I'd have to get something for her. I could buy her something and not worry if she got me something. I'll have to remember that.

"What kind of things?"

She put them under and around her tree.

"And I don't want you digging through them. You don't like Christmas, remember?"

I waved my hand at her.

"Yeah, yeah."

"Oh, by the way, Yvonne Barnett is due to come in this morning."

"Did you tell me?"

"Uh, yes, I did."

I looked at her.

"Uh-huh," I said and went into my office.

I finished my breakfast and carried the bottle to the can and dropped it in.

"Nothing but net," I said.

I finished the paper and went to the window when I heard a knock on my door.

I turned to see Yvonne Barnett standing there. She didn't barge in like Neda. I liked her already.

"Mr. Cameron?"

I walked over to her.

"Mrs. Barnett, please come in."

She didn't look eighty-two, but if you have her kind of money, you could look any age you wanted. She moved with the grace one would expect from a lady of her means.

"My secretary said you wanted to speak with me," she said sitting across from the desk.

"Yes, I hope I'm not imposing on your time. I know you must be busy at…right now."

"If you mean Edwin's business, it is being taken care of. We are reorganizing the company to put a new CEO in place, but I will answer whatever questions you have, and I hope you can answer whatever questions I have."

"I hope so, Mrs. Barnett."

"Where shall we start?"

"I'm curious about one thing. Why did you want me on this case?"

"Did you know my son?"

"Only through the news."

"Mr. Cameron—"

"Lee. Please call me, Lee."

"Lee. My son followed your career."

I leaned back. She could see the surprise on my face.

"Why?"

"Edwin liked Clint Eastwood. He liked the Dirty Harry movies and always said we need more police officers like that. To him, you were that type. Maybe not that extreme, but one that bent the rules a little."

"Well, Mrs. Barnett, I'm flattered, but my actions, if you will, made me leave the force before I was ready. The powers that be didn't like Dirty Harry."

"I'll leave that between you and the police department."

"Jack Vincent told me you wanted the investigation hush hush. Has it been satisfactory so far?"

"Yes."

"Let me tell you where we stand, and I would like to ask you some questions."

"Good."

I told her about the talks with Philo Griggs, Xavier Unger, Ira Quint and Isaac Kruger. I told her we talked to Doreen Tilly, and I compared notes with Ollie.

"Do you think Isaac Kruger would kill your son?"

"No, that's preposterous. You wasted your time with him. He's a big blow hard, but he's not a murderer."

"A lot of people who you wouldn't expect to commit murder when stressed or pressed into a corner will do exactly that if it comes down to it."

"I'll bet my company on Isaac's innocence."

"Why would your daughter-in-law want me to question him?"

"Neda is interested in Edwin's life insurance. She probable wanted you to find Edwin's killer so she could collect the insurance. I never believed she loved him, but that's neither here nor there."

"What about Philo Griggs?"

"The man was a thief, but I had no problem with him. We treated each other with respect, and I liked him, but a thief is a thief. I don't blame Edwin for firing him."

"What about the jail time?"

"I would have tried to talk Edwin out of that, but Philo was also dealing drugs. I don't approve of that."

"Did Edwin and Neda get along?"

"As much as a man and a wife young enough to be his daughter can get along."

"I take it you didn't approve of their marriage."

"No, I didn't."

"Do you think she had a lover on the side?"

"I don't know, but it wouldn't surprise me."

"Do you know where she went on her out of town trips? I understand she left the country at least once a month."

"That's right, but I don't know where she went. I've heard down to the Caribbean somewhere."

"Edwin never mentioned it?"

"Not to me. He knew I didn't approve of her, so we didn't talk about her too much."

"Have you given any thought to who might want to kill your son?"

"No."

"Any business deals that went wrong? Something that would make someone want to get even?"

"Our company makes deals all the time. Not all work out, but I don't think any would be bad enough for murder."

"Any questions for me?"

"Do you have any leads past the ones you told me?"

"Not at the moment. I stay in contact with Detective Fletcher. We bang our heads together to see what's new."

A little lie didn't hurt if it pleased her.

"Did Edwin meet with anyone that appeared strange to you?" I asked. "Someone who didn't quite fit in with the rest. Someone you thought looked out of place."

"What do you mean?"

"You may not know this, but did he carry on any business he wouldn't want anyone to know about?"

She bit her lower lip.

"Not that I know of. Why?"

"Jack Vincent told me you didn't want the Barnett name dragged through the mud."

"That is correct."

I drummed my fingers on the desk.

"Out with it," she said.

"What if he was?"

"What if he was what?"

"What if he was doing something that would blacken the eye of the company and your name? What if he was doing something so dreadful, he wouldn't talk to anyone about it? What if he was doing something he felt he should carry to his grave?"

"I don't know what you mean?"

"What if I turn up something in that regard? What do I do?"

She sat quiet. I could see the wheels spinning behind those eyes, but her eyes didn't give anything away.

"Mr. Cameron, if you find anything that horrible, I expect you to notify the police of it and notify me."

"I will."

I let out a sigh of relief. I don't know why I was so relieved. It could have been that I knew where I stood with her. I don't know why that mattered, but at the time it did.

"Anything else you'd like to discuss?" I asked.

"Not at the moment."

I stood and put out my hand.

"It has been a pleasure to meet you, Mrs. Barnett. I assure you I will find who killed your son and I'm sure the police would tell you the same thing."

"Thank you, Lee. If you need anything from me or anyone at the company, please let me know."

"Does that include Neda?"

"It includes everybody. If you have a problem with her, you let me know."

She stood and I showed her to the door. A man in a chauffeur's uniform sat with Sheila. They talked like great friends.

He stood when she came in.

"Thank you again, Mr. Cameron," she said smiling.

"My pleasure."

He opened the door and they left with her arm hooked in his.

That evening Sheila and I sat around eating her chicken gumbo. I didn't know the girl could cook that good. My preference is to eat it like a gravy, not soupy, which is the norm, over rice with potato salad on the side.

"What was your opinion of Yvonne Barnett?" she asked.

I stuffed my mouth with potato salad.

"Is this your last meal?" she asked putting down her spoon and watching me.

"No. Why?"

"You don't have to choke yourself. Nobody'll take it from you."

I swallowed and wiped my mouth.

"I like her better than Neda."

"Did you get anything out of her you can use?"

"I asked her about Griggs and Kruger. She said she'd bet her company on Kruger's innocence."

"What about Philo Griggs? Would she bet the company on him?"

"I don't think so. She liked him. Said they got along great. She said she would have tried to talk Edwin out of jail time if it was only the theft, but he was dealing."

"Seems awful lenient for someone who wields that much power."

"I don't see her as a power monger. Everyone around knows she's in charge. She doesn't need to beat them over the head with it, but then again, I don't know what goes on behind company doors."

"Wipe your chin."

I did. "Did you get along with her chauffeur?"

She smiled.

"What's so funny?"

"He's quite a gent. I found him interesting. I don't think he's the chauffeur."

"He dressed like one."

"The way he talked led me to believe he's more. Maybe they do that so as not to attract attention and he liked my decorations."

My turn to smile.

"So, what's next?"

I took a couple of bites before she grabbed the spoon from me.

"I'll get back with Ollie next week. I'd like to have this cleared up by Christmas."

"You don't have any new leads. How can you?"

"I'll go back and brow beat the ones we talked to. Maybe something new will pop up."

"You might want to start with Doreen Tilly."

"Why?"

"Didn't you say you didn't think she was telling you everything she knew? If you talk to her again, she might spill something."

I pointed at her. "Good idea. That's why I keep you around. And the cooking. And the…well, you know."

She smiled.

"Oh," she said, "would you go check my mail. I forgot."

She handed me the key to her mailbox.

I had to work the key to get it open. Nothing there. I guess no one liked her.

On the way back to her apartment I went by my car to make sure it was secure for the night.

But it wasn't.

All four tires were cut. I went to the road like I would be able to see the slasher making his escape.

My heart raced. If the killer was the one who cut the tires, and who else would it be, it was another message. He knew where I went and worse, he knew where Sheila lived. That scared me more than anything.

I ran upstairs and threw the keys on the table.

"Where's my mail?"

"Nothing there."

I paced around the room.

"What's the matter?"

I stopped and faced her.

"Someone cut my tires."

"Are you sure they were cut?"

"Yes. All four tires don't just go flat all at the same time. Besides when you see slits on the sides, that's a sure sign they were cut."

"Yes, I guess you're right."

"You can't stay here!"

"Why?"

"He knows where you live. He could do something to you."

"I'm not leaving my home."

"Come stay with me til we get this guy."

"No. I will not let this thug scare me."

"You telling me you're not scared?"

She thought then said, "Of course, I'm scared. I'm not used to this."

I could see she would stand her ground.

"Remember what I told you about the guy when Crystal and I had our fight?"

"Yes."

She pulled up her sleeves to show me her forearms.

"Remember the story about these?"

"Yes."

"I've already been through hell. One more time won't hurt."

"Hurt? It could get you killed."

"You're overreacting."

I went to the window and looked down at my car.

"He probably followed us here. He could bust in anytime."

I turned to her.

"What would you do if that happened?"

She shrugged.

"I'll stay here, then," I said.

"How will you find him if you're hanging around here? And I need to go to work."

She came to me. I hugged her.

"It will be all right," she said. "I'll be okay."

"It's against my better judgment."

"You don't have better judgment," she said kissing my ear.

"Stop that," I said, "I'm trying to think."

"Think later. Come on."

She took my hand.

"Wait," I said, "I need to call Ollie."

She patiently waited while we talked.

"He will put a patrol around the complex," I said when I hung up.

"How will that help?"

"Maybe the show of cops will keep him away."

"Maybe, but I doubt it."

I threw up my hands.

"What do you suggest?"

"I suggest we go about our business. Show him he can't scare us, even if he does. Anyway, he can come around and hide when he sees the patrol car. They can't be here around the clock."

"I don't know."

"You might as well know. I'm not budging. I will live here and I will go to work and I will go about my business as usual…I'll only do it more carefully."

"What will I do with you?"

"Support me. Be there when I need you."

What could I do? Tie her down and throw her in a closet. I'd rather face the killer.

She took my hand again. This time I gave in.

9

Tuesday, December 14th

I was still cussing whoever cut my tires. I couldn't have them repaired. Oh, no, he cut them enough to make me buy new ones. That put a dent into Neda Barnett's fee.

Sheila was at her desk and didn't look none too happy. Some of her perpetual Christmas spirit was gone. I did a quick inventory of the weekend to make sure I was still in her good graces. I couldn't think of anything I did, but that didn't mean anything.

So, I dove in.

"Good morning!" I said.

She saw through my phony greeting.

"Why are you so chipper?" she asked.

"Why are you in a bad mood?"

She nodded in the direction of my office.

"You have a visitor. It's her."

I looked at the closed door.

"Which her?" I tried to keep my voice down.

"Crystal Hudson, the bitch."

"Oh," I said. "I thought I had screwed up along the way this weekend."

She forced a smile. "No, you didn't."

"Did you play nice with her?"

"Let's just say I wasn't rude."

I patted her on the head.

"Good girl."

She mumbled something as I went into my office. I'm probably better off not knowing what she said.

Crystal was standing at the window in my usual spot. She turned when I came in.

"What do I owe this to?" I asked going to the frig for breakfast.

She was smiling and held a large brown envelope. I figured she was up to something or already had done something.

I sat at my desk. She sat in the guest's chair.

"Aren't you going to offer me one" she said pointing at the bottle.

"Would you like one?" I offered holding up the bottle.

"No thanks."

Women.

"Do you know where Neda Barnett has been the last few days?" she asked grinning like the Cheshire cat.

"Should I?"

"It wouldn't hurt."

Her grin couldn't get any bigger.

"Let's see," I said rubbing my chin and looking at her. "Someone in this room knows where she was and that someone ought to say what's on her mind before her teeth fall out."

She tapped the envelope on her lap.

"Neda Barnett left town a couple of days ago. I—"

"How did you know she was leaving town?"

"I have ways. I am a pretty good reporter."

"That's what I hear. Continue."

"I wanted to see if she was up to no good. I went back and checked the times she was out of town. Every time she left, it was big news, but only because she married money. You know how people are. They want to know what the wealthy are doing like they can identify with it."

I took a sip from the bottle and listened.

"I decided to take a ride out to her house," Crystal said. "Out of curiosity I parked down the street where I could see her driveway. Just when I was about to give up and go home, her car pulls out of the driveway with the lights off. I—"

I held up my hand.

"What time was this?"

"Around eleven, maybe eleven-thirty. I wondered why the lights were off. She was sneaking off. I didn't see why it would matter to anyone around there if she left town or not. I don't know what kind of neighbors she has. They may not care, or they may. I followed the car and almost lost it until the lights came on. I followed the car all the way to the airport and parked behind it. I tried to talk to her when she got out, but a big guy ushered me away from her until she was inside then he went in with the luggage."

I finished the bottle and put the cap on but decided to let it rest on the desk.

"Did she have a lot of luggage?"

"A couple of suitcases and a couple of small bags. Judging from past trips she only stayed a few days and usually on a weekend. If my information is correct, she should have been back late last night or early this morning."

She smiled that big smile again.

"What now?"

"I found out where she went."

"Tell me before I bust and get Dr. Pepper all over you."

"Jamaica."

She tapped the envelope again just to remind me she knew something I didn't.

"I have a friend who works at the resort she went to. She and one of her friends took some pictures and sent them to me. I owe them now."

"I hope it was worth it."

"Oh, I believe so and you'll be interested in it, too."

"Why?"

"She was with a male companion."

My eyes lifted a little."

"Anyone we know?"

She nodded. The ends of her smile must have touched behind her head.

"Are you going to let me see those or will you tease me all morning?"

She took one photo out and put it face down on her lap then handed me the envelope.

"What's that?" I asked.

"You see this one last."

There were about ten or fifteen pictures in the envelope.

"Are they in any kind of order?"

"No."

I went through them.

Neda Barnett coming off the plane in Kingston. She wore sunglasses and a flattering outfit.

"She'd look good in anything she wore," I said.

There she was checking into the hotel. Now she was sitting in the dining room. This one must have been later because she had changed her clothes. She faced the camera. A large man sat across from her. I couldn't see his face.

Another one of the pair walking hand in hand on the beach. Again, their backs were to the camera. She almost had on her swimsuit or whatever you call something women wear to show off their assets. The man had on a pair of baggy shorts. I could see the love handles trying to dive off the side.

There she was lying on her back stretched out on a towel. I figured she would have more covered if she didn't have anything on. There was an empty towel next to hers. I guessed Love Handles was probably in the water or working up a sweat somewhere.

The rest was of the pair at different times, but none showed the faces.

"Okay, she has a male friend, or boyfriend, or whatever. I'm not really surprised, but it looks to me she could have done better. I'm sure there a lot of young studs running around Jamaica."

She handed me the last one.

I looked at the picture a good thirty seconds then up at Crystal. She nodded and smiled.

I looked back down. Neda Barnett and Isaac Kruger were walking along the beach. He had his arm around her waist just under her breast. Her face showed no expression. I couldn't tell if she was enjoying the moment. Kruger had a grin to match Crystal's. Why wouldn't he enjoy it? He had a woman young enough to be his daughter and it was legal.

"Your friend took these, right?" I asked recovering from my shock.

"Right."

"And these are recent?"

"Right."

"This is after Edwin Barnett had met his maker?"

"Right."

"Is this the first time they were together?"

She shook her head and smiled.

"I wish you would quit smiling like that."

"I can't help it."

"That bitch lied to me and she knows what I told her if she lied to me."

"What are you going to do?"

I got up, grabbed the empty bottle and slammed it in the trash can then threw open the door.

Sheila spun around.

"What's the matter?"

"Get hold of Neda Barnett and Isaac Kruger. Tell them I want them both here now. Don't tell them they will be together. I want them to be surprised. Tell them if I have to, I'll come down there and drag their asses over here. Don't take no for an answer."

I slammed the door and collapsed in my chair. They looked at me from the picture apparently enjoying the ruse they played on me.

"Damn it," I said straightening up the pictures and put them back in the envelope.

"Keep them," Crystal said when I handed it back to her. "I have plenty of copies."

I took the last picture and slipped it in my desk drawer.

"Thanks," I said.

"Can I print anything? This is going to be a good story."

"I don't think so."

"Why?"

"You remember what we talked about the first time?"

"Yes."

"You remember what I told you about Yvonne Barnett not wanting anything to harm the family name?"

"Yes."

I tapped the envelope.

"You know what she would do if she saw these pictures? Her daughter-in-law running around with her son's former friend. What do you think that would do to their good name?"

"Come on, Cameron. I did this myself."

"Tell you what, Crystal. I'll let you know after I talk to these two birds. I want to get it from their mouths. I want to see their expressions when I show them these pictures and I want them to try to explain it."

She sat back pouting.

"I have something you can print," I said.

"What?"

"Someone cut all my tires last night."

She took out her pad and wrote something."

"Where were you?"

"That's not important."

She looked up and smiled.

"It's not what you think."

"I wasn't thinking anything."

"Bull. Women are always thinking something. You can print that. No, not that. You can print what I told you about the tires."

She smiled again and put her pad away.

Sheila came in.

"Mr. Kruger is on the phone. He said he can't come in today."

I punched the line and picked up the receiver.

"Mr. Kruger, I need to see you in my office as soon as you can get here…I don't care what your previous engagements are…I'll go down there and drag your fat ass up here if I have to…Call whoever you damn well please."

I slammed the phone down.

"What about Neda Barnett?"

"She said she'll be here shortly."

"Thanks."

The two women looked at each other. I thought I saw the ice crack between them. They would want to know the outcome.

I was on the phone with Jack Vincent when Neda Barnett came in. Isaac Kruger had called him raising hell over my demand.

"I'll call you back," I said.

"I hope you have a good reason for this," she said.

"Please take a seat," I said motioning to the chair. She didn't look any worse for wear so soon after returning.

"What is this about?"

"We have one more person coming then will get started."

She reached into her purse then changed her mind. Probably for a cigarette.

I heard the outer open and slam. Isaac Kruger burst in.

"You better have a good reason for this or—"

He saw Neda.

"Or what, Mr. Kruger?"

"Nothing," he said waving his hand.

Sheila came in with her pad.

"Miss Arceneaux will take the minutes of this meeting," I said. "I'm really sure you know each other so we'll get started."

I showed them the envelope.

"Mrs. Barnett, you gave me Mr. Kruger's name as a possible suspect in the murder of your husband. Is that correct?"

"I guess so."

"I think a more appropriate answer would be yes. Don't you think?"

She looked at Kruger.

"Yes."

"Mr. Kruger knows about that because we discussed it."

"I don't think you have the right—"

"Well, I do, and you pretended to hate her, called her some name."

She looked at him.

"Now, Mrs. Barnett, why did you tell me Mr. Kruger would want to kill your husband?"

"You wanted names."

"Yes, I wanted names. I told you reliable names. Do you really think Mr. Kruger killed your husband?"

"No. You satisfied?"

"Not quite."

Sheila's hand moved swiftly across the page. I was proud of her. I think she was enjoying this.

"Mrs. Barnett," I continued, "do you remember what I told you if you lied to me?"

"Yes."

"What?"

"You'd help the police prove something or other."

I opened the envelope and took out the pictures.

"I have something to show you."

I handed the stack to Neda Barnett. Kruger looked on. They went through the stack without comment or showing any emotion.

"Needless to say," I said taking back the photos, "we know who the woman is, but who is the man?"

Kruger jumped to his feet.

"SIT DOWN!" I said standing.

Sheila and Neda jumped.

"I'll sue you for everything you've got," Kruger said, but he sat down.

"You do what you have to do. I don't have anything. Now, who is the man?"

"I don't know," Kruger said.

"A friend," Neda said.

I opened the desk and showed them the picture with Kruger facing the camera.

"It looks like he's a very good friend."

Neda put her hand to her mouth in a show of surprise. Kruger did nothing.

"Will one of you tell me what this is all about?"

"We met in Jamaica," Kruger said.

"Obviously," I said putting the pictures back in the envelope.

I could feel Sheila smiling.

"Why did you send me chasing the wind, Mrs. Barnett?"

"I...I couldn't think of anyone else. You were pressuring me for names."

"What about you, Mr. Kruger? Don't you mind this? Aren't you afraid of your reputation?"

"No, I didn't mind. It's no big deal to me. So, what if everyone knows about me and her. Do you think they will care? It's no one's business, but ours."

"Maybe not to you, but I don't think this Mrs. Barnett would like the other Mrs. Barnett to see these pictures."

Neda sat up.

"No, you can't do that," she said.

I sat back.

"You made a fool of me," I said. "You came to me. You want me to find your husband's killer because you said you wanted more eyes out there. What's your game?"

"I don't have a game."

I leaned forward and intertwined my fingers.

"Did you and Mr. Kruger conspire to kill your husband?"

"WE DID NOT," she said.

"That's ridiculous," Kruger said. "I don't have to put up with this."

He turned to Neda.

"And you don't have to, either."

They got up to leave.

"One more question, Mrs. Barnett."

"Don't answer anything," Kruger said taking her arm.

"No, I'll answer."

"Am I to assume Mr. Kruger is no longer a suspect?"

"Yes, and you're off the case."

"Wrong," I said. "I'm still on it, but I'm not working for you anymore, but I'll keep your money."

"You can't—," Kruger started.

She put a hand on his arm.

"It's okay," she said.

When they got to the door she turned.

"You won't show those to Yvonne, will you?"

I shrugged.

"We'll see where this takes the investigation. If I don't have to, I won't."

She looked at Sheila.

"Do I get a copy of those minutes? I want to make sure my words don't get twisted."

I turned to Sheila.

"What do you have there?"

She held up the pad so Neda Barnett and Isaac Kruger could see it. All that was on it was few words.

"My Christmas list," she said.

"Bastard," Neda said and stormed off with Kruger hot on her heels.

10

Monday, December 20th

I spoke with Jack the day after I met with Neda Barnett and Isaac Kruger. He and Ursula were very unhappy with me for treating a prominent attorney like I did. Everything was smoothed out. At least they hadn't heard from Yvonne Barnett. I didn't expect them to…or hoped they wouldn't.

Things had calmed down on the Edwin Barnett murder investigation front. I guess even cops and criminals take time off for the holidays. I didn't have anything new. Neither did Ollie. It appeared everything was at a standstill for the time being. The older Mrs. Barnett wouldn't be happy with that. She would be celebrating, if you wanted to call it that, Christmas for a long time without her son. How would she handle it? I could guess how Neda would handle it.

Sheila was in the Christmas spirit more as the time neared. She took to wearing Christmassy clothes and jewelry. Some days she wore her Santa Claus hat. Who knew what she would burst in with today with the big day being only five days away?

I was standing at the window when she came in. The hat was in place. Her green and red sweater had a Santa holding a large candy cane rushing through the sky. Rudolph's nose was a small blinking red light.

"The light is a nice touch," I said.

She patted it and smiled.

"It's in the right place, over my heart."

The number of shoppers had grown steadily over the past week. I didn't see the young muggers scoping out victims. I guess they're taking the holidays off, too.

"Isn't it exciting?" she asked hooking her arm through mine.

"Very."

"Look at all those people," she said. "Hustling. Bustling. Shopping."

I thought I recognized the little old lady who got mugged.

"I know you don't like the season. Why don't you tell me why?"

I tightened my grip on her arm.

"I used to love it. When we were kids, we'd help my parents decorate the tree. My dad gave us instructions on how to put the icicles on. He didn't want us just throwing them on. They had to be placed and not on the wires, but on the branches and needles. Then we took it down New Year's Day.

"My mom was a wonderful cook. We ate pretty good those days between Thanksgiving and New Year's. My dad made the best fudge and lemon meringue pies. He beat the meringue by hand with a fork. Sometimes he would let us help but watched to make sure we did it right."

"Then we grew up and moved out. We had holidays with them, but it wasn't the same. I guess things change and your outlook changes when you grow up. Anyway, the excitement I used to feel gradually disappeared.

"Then when they died, I lost interest all together. I didn't even put up a tree or shop. I didn't feel anything about the holidays. They were just another few weeks in my life. In fact, I looked forward to the end so everything could back to normal."

"Well, you have me, now," she said kissing my cheek. "You can have good holidays again."

"As long as you enjoy it and judging from your—"

Something didn't feel right. The hair on the back of my neck stood up. It was down in the street. That's where my eyes went. Although everything looked okay, it didn't feel that way to me.

I tried to push Sheila aside, but she didn't realize what was going on and kept her arm hooked in mine. I couldn't get it free.

She screamed when the glass shattered. Large pieces flew into her face and neck. The bullet grazed her shoulder and spun her around. I heard the thud as it hit the wall behind us. She fell on the wounded shoulder and screamed even louder. Blood covered the side of her face and the floor.

I looked through the broken glass to see if I could see anything unusual. I only saw people looking around and pointing towards where I was standing in the window.

I bent down to check her out. The face and neck wounds looked worse than her shoulder wound. I picked her up and headed for the hospital, but of course, I had trouble getting the door open with her in my arms.

"Lee," she cried.

"Don't talk. I'm taking you to the hospital."

I put her in the passenger front seat and rushed into the traffic on Shelberg Drive. I heard honking and shouting, but it sounded distant, and I didn't care. Swerving through the traffic I made the four blocks to Marie Paige Memorial Hospital in no time.

Two attendants pushed her into the emergency room. They worked to stop the bleeding. They said she was losing consciousness.

A doctor came in, looked her over, and took her to the operating room. A nurse showed me where I could wait.

I sat there, stunned. Everything I did and said appeared to be blurred. I don't remember any of it. My shirt was full of blood, but I didn't care. I wanted to cry but didn't.

What if she died? I couldn't sit so I paced the room. Others came and went. I'm sure they were put off by the blood, but I didn't think about it.

Finally, I sat back down and put my head in my hands.

"You can cry if you want."

I looked up to see Crystal Hudson.

"News travels fast," I said.

"We're a newspaper. We know everything."

She sat next to me.

"How you doing?"

"Better than Sheila."

"You talk to anyone yet?"

I shook my head.

"How long has it been?"

I leaned back.

"God, Crystal, I don't even know. It was like time stopped. One minute we were at the window in my office talking about Christmas and the next…here."

"I…I don't know what to say, Lee."

"What can you say?"

"What can I do?"

"Nothing right now. We can't do anything but wait."

I stood and walked to the doorway.

"Wait for the news."

I turned to her.

"She didn't deserve this. She didn't do anything to anyone."

"It probably was meant for you."

"I know. I tried to push her out of the way, but she wouldn't move. She was hanging on to my arm."

Crystal came up to me.

"She loves you, Lee. There's no telling how long she's been waiting to hear you say that."

"Yeah. Love. Look where it got her."

"It's not love that put her here."

"Then what is it?"

She shrugged.

"I don't really know, but it could have happened anywhere the shooter chose. He knows who you are. Sheila, too. The problem is you don't know who he is."

"If she'd only let go of my arm, I could've pushed her out of the way."

"Well, it didn't happen that way. Don't beat yourself up over it. She'll need you."

"I figured she knew how I felt about her."

"Women like to hear it. Remember that."

"I'll try."

"I have an offer."

"What's that?"

"If she needs somewhere to stay while she's recovering, she can stay with me. I have plenty of room."

"If she recovers."

"She will. Think positive."

I smiled.

"She told me why she uh, dislikes, you so much. We talked about her getting over it. This could give her a chance. I'll tell her. Thanks."

She kissed me on the cheek.

"You're welcome. I have to go. I'll check with you later."

I nodded and watched her walk down the hall. She met Ollie and Tom. They talked for a while and kept moving.

"How you doing, buddy," Ollie said hugging me.

Tom gave me a stiff handshake.

"Okay. A little in shock, I guess."

"You remember what I told you?" Tom asked.

"You mean about the killer would have no problem killing me."

He nodded.

"I guess it's true," I said going back to the couch.

They sat on each side of me.

"Looks like our boy is getting bold," Ollie said. "Shooting in the middle of a crowd."

"He may think you're getting close," Tom said.

"Too close," I said. "You been to my office?"

"The guys are there, now. They'll send the slug to ballistics. We'll find out if it came from the same rifle that killed Barnett."

"What was it?" Tom asked.

"A Remington 700. 30-06."

"Popular model," Tom said. "It could belong to anyone in this area who hunts or just likes to shoot guns."

Ollie nodded.

An older couple came in and sat across the room. She was in a wheelchair; he used a walker. She had a box of tissues in her lap and dabbed at her eyes. He held her hand and talked to her, but we couldn't hear.

"I wonder if I'll live to be that old," I said.

"What?" Ollie asked.

"Look at them. I don't know what the problem is, but people that old shouldn't have to go through whatever it is they're going through."

I sat and watched the old couple. They looked to be suffering.

A middle-aged couple came in and went over to them. The woman bent over and told them something. Both started crying. It looked like they let everything go. I figured they were the older couple's children. All four left the room. All four were crying. They didn't notice us.

"Sad," Tom said.

I jumped up when the doctor came in. He carried something.

"Mr. Cameron?"

"I'm Lee Cameron."

He put out his hand and told me his name, which I don't remember. I don't even know if I heard it.

He looked at Tom and Ollie.

"I need to talk you."

"Doctor, this is Oliver Fletcher with the Shelberg Police Department and Tom Jones, owner of The 10th Inning. You can say whatever you need to say in front of them. They're my good friends."

"Okay. Miss Arceneaux will be all right. We have her in recovery."

My knees turned to jelly and I collapsed on the couch.

He squatted in front of me.

"She'll be there a while then we'll move her to a room. Why don't you go home? Change your clothes, get some rest. With any luck she'll be in a room this evening."

He handed me Sheila's Christmas sweater. Rudolph's nose was still blinking. He was a tough little guy, too.

"I took a lot of glass out of her face and neck," the doctor said. "A lot of shards in her shoulder, but not so much in her face. It should heal nicely without any scars. The shards cut into the shoulder muscle so she will have to take it easy for a while. The shards did more damage than the bullet. It just grazed her shoulder."

He stood to leave. "She's a lucky young lady. You got her here in time for us to catch the major damage and treat it without any more significant problems. Just keep her quiet for a while."

"Thanks, Doc," I said standing to shake his hand.

He patted me on the shoulder.

"I better get back."

Then I flopped back in the chair and cried. My friends let me.

"Sorry," I said wiping my eyes.

"Why?" Tom asked. "You don't have anything to be sorry for."

"You need to do what the doc said," Ollie said. "Go home and change. Take a shower then come back. You'll feel better."

I nodded. That was all I could do.

We walked out together and split up in the parking lot.

"Thanks, guys," I said and went to my car.

The blood in my car would have to wait to get cleaned. I took a shower and changed. Instead of washing my bloody shirt, I threw it in the trash. I spread Sheila's sweater out on the kitchen counter. Rudolph smiled at me like everything was normal.

I laid down but couldn't sleep. I just stared at the ceiling thinking about Sheila. I smiled at her numerous retorts and her smile; a smile that told me when to quit acting the idiot or shut up. She was good for me and I didn't notice.

"Women want to hear it," Crystal had said.

"I love you, Sheila," I said to the ceiling, but it didn't answer.

I must have dozed off because when I woke up, it was dark out. The clock said six.

I straightened up and drove back to the hospital.

I checked with the desk, and they gave me her room number. The doc had left a message that I could see her when I came back.

A nurse was in the room with her. Sheila was asleep with a tube in her arm. Her face and neck were bandaged.

The nurse smiled when I told her who I was.

"I'll leave you alone, but she'll probably sleep the rest of the night."

"Thanks."

She turned when she got to the door.

"Mr. Cameron, I didn't see anything if you would like to spend the night. It may not be comfortable, but you're welcome to it."

She winked at me and left.

I pulled the chair up to the bed and took her hand without the tube.

"You're going to be okay. The doc said you would and he wouldn't lie."

I stood and kissed her forehead then her lips. They were so soft. Were they always that soft? How many times had I kissed her lips? Hundreds, maybe thousands. Sometimes passionate, but mostly just a peck here and there. But did I really notice how soft and inviting there were? No, not really. Just another thing I took for granted.

"I'll notice from now on," I said.

I put my head on her hand.

"I'll notice everything you do. I haven't been very attentive. I don't know how you can care, much less love, a man like me. I—"

Something moved.

I looked up to see her looking at me.

"Sheila," I whispered. "I'm so sorry."

She stroked my cheek and shook her head.

"Nu…nu…nothing to be…sor…sorry for."

Her eyes closed.

I could feel the tears streaming down my cheeks. I didn't try to wipe them away.

"Rest," I said when I regained my composure.

She nodded but didn't open her eyes.

"I'll see you tomorrow," I said and kissed her on the lips, those soft lips.

I stood looking at her. I didn't want to leave her, but I needed to go home and rest. There were things I needed to do, and I would need my strength. Standing at the door I clenched and relaxed my fists and did it over and over. I wanted to hit something or somebody. I wanted to hit the person who shot her. I looked at her for a long time then left.

I called Ollie when I was in the car.

"This slug matched the one that killed Edwin Barnett. The same gun shot both."

"Thanks," I said and hung up.

I grabbed the steering wheel so tight my knuckles turned white. I wanted to kill this guy for what he did to Sheila. Edwin Barnett was pushed from my mind. This had become personal. I wanted revenge for Sheila.

I forced myself to relax. As bad as I wanted to get my hands on her assailant, I had to let the system run its course. I didn't want to do something that would let him free on a technicality.

The only problem I had with the system is that it grinds so damn slow.

11

Tuesday, December 21st

I went by the office on my way to the hospital to see if we had any messages or threatening letters. Tom had spoken with the bank and had the window repaired. I had forgotten all about it. I thanked him, which of course, wouldn't be near enough. We'd settle up later.

I called Jack and told him I wanted to talk to him and Ursula today. He could tell I was upset and said he'd be in whenever I was ready.

"Together," I told him. "I want both of you together."

"Okay, Okay, Lee. Settle down. Come in after lunch. I'll get her here one way or another."

I hung up.

Sheila was awake, but groggy. I'd take groggy over dead any day. Her mostly untouched breakfast tray was off to the side.

At least she smiled when she saw me.

"How are you doing?" I asked.

"Does a girl have to get shot to get this much attention from you?"

"Not anymore."

I kissed her forehead and sat down. The chair was where I left it the night before.

"I'm sorry, Sheila. I shouldn't have let you—"

She put her hand to my lips.

"You didn't know."

"I told you it could be dangerous, but I should have left you out."

"You're the one who needs to worry. Anyway, you couldn't leave me out. I work with you. I'm guilty by association"

She closed her eyes. I thought she'd go back to sleep.

"That guy is still out there," she said without opening them. "He'll try again. You have to be careful."

"I...I'm glad you're okay. I'm going to see Jack and Ursula after lunch."

Her eyes popped open.

"Don't do anything rash. Don't lose your head. And don't say anything you'll regret later."

"Okay. Did the doc say when you'll be up and around?"

"He wants me to stay here for a couple of days."

"You can't stay by yourself when you get out."

"Why?"

"You'll need someone to help you?"

"To do what?"

I threw up my hands.

"I don't know. Things."

"What kind of things?"

"I don't know, Sheila."

"I can take of myself, thank you."

"Well, I can see you're getting better. I don't want you staying by yourself. That...that...whoever tried to kill whichever one he was aiming at may try again."

She didn't say anything. I didn't know if that was good or bad.

"Crystal said you could stay at her place until you're better."

"Why would I want to do that?"

"Look, she offered. She said she has plenty of room. I thought it was good gesture, but it's up to you."

"No."

I bent down to get close to her.

"I care about you," I said. "Take her up on it at least until I catch this guy. I'll feel better."

"How long will it take you to catch this guy, Sherlock?"

"I will put all my energy to find him so we can get back to normal."

"Normal? What's normal?"

"Look, Christmas is coming. I'll bet Crystal has her place decorated like you do." I stood up. "Who knows? You two might hit it off. You can talk about your problem with her. You can renew your friendship."

She took a deep breath.

"I'm tired," she said and closed her eyes.

"Okay, I'll go and let you rest."

I went to the door.

"Lee," she said.

"Yeah?"

"I'll think about it."

"Okay."

It was early, but I went to the station. I knew Ollie would be there. I didn't want to go to the office or to my apartment.

"Hey, old buddy," he said when I walked into his office. "How's Sheila?"

I flopped down in the chair by his desk.

"Good. Nothing life threatening. Hopefully she can go home in a few days."

"You tell her you love her?"

"What?"

"You tell her you love her? Sometimes things like this bring out our true feelings."

"Are you Dr. Phil or Dear Abby?"

"Neither. I'm a guy who knows what it's like to truly love a woman and tell her often. You should do the same. That girl really cares for you."

"I don't know if I'm worth it."

He waved his hand.

"Cut the crap. We're all worth it. Some people need more work, that's all."

"I guess."

"Now, on to business. Jack told me you wanted to speak with him and Ursula. What about?"

"About what happened."

"What do you plan to tell them?"

I shrugged.

"Let me give you some pointers. They know how you feel. I'll bet you're busting at the gut to get your hands on this guy. Am I correct?"

"Yes."

"Don't go off half-cocked. This guy's laying for you. He missed once, but he may not miss again. You go off crazed by what happened and you won't be able to concentrate. You'll get yourself killed and I'll have to do this by myself. Understand?"

"Yeah, I understand."

"I hope you don't go into that meeting ranting and raving about revenge and that sort of stuff. It won't get you anywhere."

"Ollie, do you think he'll try to get to Sheila?"

"That's possible if he can find her. Threatening someone's family, or in your case, Sheila, then carrying it out can have a profound effect on the hunter and the hunted. The hunted, our killer, will be braver. He knows he shook you up. The hunter, you, is shaken to the point where you may make a big mistake because you're letting your emotions come into play. Does that make any sense?"

I nodded.

"Good."

"He knows where she lives."

"She needs to go somewhere else."

"Crystal offered to let her stay with her. She said she'd think about it."

"Then make her do it."

"Make her? You don't make her do anything."

He looked at me. I could tell that look.

"I told Jack I'd sit in on the meeting. Okay with you?"

"Sure."

"Let's compare notes on what we have so far."

We huddled around his desk. One of the other detectives gave us some old doughnuts left over since breakfast. I didn't realize how hungry I was.

Jack and Ursula were waiting on us. She looked impatient with having to meet with me or us. Jack wiped his brow.

"Please get on with it, Mr. Cameron," Ursula said.

"I know you're busy, Madam DA, so I'll get right to the point."

Ollie gave me the look that said rein it in.

"Yesterday, my secretary was shot. Ambushed while we stood in my office. She is the proverbial innocent bystander."

"How is she doing?" Ursula asked.

"Well, thank you for asking. She may go home in a couple of days."

"That's good," Jack said.

"I believe the bullet was meant for me. We had two other incidences where we received messages from the killer."

Ursula sat up.

"What kind? Why wasn't I told?"

Jack turned to her.

"You weren't told because we are working the case, Ursula. I'm not going to tell you everything that happens. In some instances, it is wise not to tell too many people what is going on."

"You mean you don't trust me?"

"It's not—", Jack started, but I cut him off.

"It doesn't matter," I said, "who knows what at this point. The killer knows I'm on the case and he has been trying different tactics to get me off. He sent a letter telling me to get off the case or someone close to me would die. I found my tires cut one morning. He's telling us he knows where we live. Now Sheila's been shot."

"What is your take on this, Detective Fletcher?" Ursula asked.

"Well, Miss Daniels, the investigation is moving slower than we hoped, but we're still working on it."

"Neda Barnett fired me," I said. "I had a talk with her and Kruger."

"Yes, I heard of that," Ursula said. "You might thank your lucky stars he didn't press charges against you."

"They both lied to me. Both intentionally misled me and that pissed me off. Isaac Kruger can do whatever he wants."

"We had an agreement," Ursula said.

"Like I said, Neda Barnett fired me, but I told her I was still on the case. Now, this has become personal."

"Lee," Jack said, "you can't be a vigilante."

"I'm not going to be a vigilante. I'll just intensify my investigation."

"What will you do if you catch him?" Ursula asked.

"When not if. That depends on him. One thing is certain. He will explain to me why he shot my secretary. You can be sure of that."

"So, you will revert to your Neanderthal tactics."

"No, ma'am, I will not revert; I never left them."

She stood up.

"Is that what you wanted to tell us? That this is personal now?"

"That's about it, but you'll get your killer. Yvonne Barnett will get off your ass and everybody will live happily ever after."

"This meeting is over, but I warn you, Mr. Cameron, don't make the Shelberg Police arrest you for excessive force."

I looked at Jack then at Ollie.

"I'll do my best."

She stormed off without as much as a good-bye or a kiss my ass.

Jack's phone rang as she slammed the door.

"Yes," he said. "I'll tell them."

"You're in luck," he said hanging up. "That was Doreen Tilly, Edwin Barnett's secretary. She said she has some information about the murder. She wants you and Detective Fletcher to go see her."

We looked at each other.

"She say what it was?" Ollie asked.

"No, she said she'd rather tell you face to face."

"Come on," Ollie said. "We'll take my car."

We met the same guard as the first time I was there. Ollie showed him his I.D. He let us through. Doreen Tilly was sitting at her desk. Nothing was on it, but a book. Looks like Yvonne Barnett's money was well spent.

She appeared nervous. Her eyes were red.

"Please sit down," she said.

"Are you all right, Miss Tilly?" Ollie asked.

"Yes and no."

"I don't understand."

She looked at me.

"I'm really sorry about Miss Arceneaux. I heard it on the news. How is she?"

"Good. Might go home in a couple of days."

"That's good."

"Did you have some information for us?" Ollie asked.

"Yes," she said, but didn't say anything.

"And it is?" I said.

She took a deep breath.

"Have you talked to Mrs. Barnett; I mean Yvonne Barnett lately?"

"I have," I said.

"Good lady. I like her a lot."

"Is there something you want to tell us?" Ollie asked. "You seem to be having a hard time getting to the point."

"Yes, I am."

She took a tissue out of her drawer and wiped her eyes then continued.

"Mr. Barnett kept a journal. I don't know why. He never told me what was in it, but he let me keep it safe. We had an agreement. If he thought he couldn't hide it, or something would happen he would call me to let me know I would have to get it. If he couldn't talk freely, he would give me a code. That code would tell me where to find it."

"It sounds like you two had an efficient system," Ollie said.

"I suppose so."

"Do you have the journal with you?"

"No, it's at my home. I'll have it here tomorrow if you want to come by and pick it up. It's locked and I didn't break into it. I didn't have the nerve. I didn't know what I'd find. I guess I really don't want to know what is in it."

She took something out of her desk drawer and pushed it to us.

"It's his cell phone," she said.

Ollie and I looked at each other.

"You took it?" I asked.

"Yes. He called me after he was shot. He gave me the code, but the code is in his cell phone, so I took it."

"That could be withholding evidence," Ollie said. "You could be in big trouble."

"I know," she said. "I know."

Then I thought of something.

"Was the phone by any chance taped under his chair with black tape?"

"Yes," she said surprised. "How did you know?"

"The day I looked through his office. I dug under his chair and found the tape. Detective Fletcher has it."

Ollie tried to bring up the call history, but it was gone.

"I erased all the calls and contacts," Doreen said.

"Do you have a key to the journal?" I asked.

"Yes, I'll have it tomorrow."

"Was Mr. Barnett up to something illegal?" Ollie asked.

"No. I don't know. I hope not."

"Was it business or personal?"

"I don't really know. You see one day he told me he was keeping a journal. It was something he felt he had to keep track of, but he didn't want anyone else to know. It was like he didn't want to get whatever he was talking about to get mixed up. It was like keeping notes or keeping records so everything would be in order."

"And he never said anything to you about what it was about?"

"No."

Ollie played with the phone a little then put it in his pocket.

"What will happen to me?" Doreen asked.

"Nothing," Ollie said.

"Nothing?"

"You helped in the investigation. You didn't know the phone could be evidence. You were protecting your boss. Let's keep it at that, but I expect you to let us know if you think of something else."

"Absolutely," she said. "I will."

She hesitated then said, "There might be one more thing."

Does this get better?

"Sometime during the summer, he started taking Friday and Monday's off. It would be the same weekend Mrs. Barnett, Neda, was out of the country. He would come back to work on the days she was expected back. He didn't tell me what was going on, and I thought that strange."

"His taking off," I asked, "or not telling you?"

"Both, really. Mr. Barnett worked a lot of weekends. Then he started taking more time off. I've been with him a long time and he would tell me things he wouldn't tell his mother or wife, but he was quiet about this. I don't know where he went or what he did. He told me if he got any calls to tell the caller he would back in four or five days and he couldn't be reached."

"Did the business suffer?" Ollie asked.

"Not that I'm aware of. When you get this high up you can take off for a few days. The lower-level people don't even know you're gone. Everything runs like it normally would."

We stood to go. She did, too.

"I hope this helps," she said.

"We'll read the journal and see if it takes us anywhere," Ollie said.

"I'll have it here tomorrow when you want to come by."

"I'll be here first thing," I said.

She nodded and we left. I could see her having a good cry through the closing elevator doors.

12

Wednesday, December 22nd

Ollie went to pick up the journal from Doreen Tilly. I went to the hospital. We would meet in Sheila's room.

She was wide awake when I walked in. Her breakfast tray was empty. Her bed was raised to a sitting position. Her face bandages were gone. All that was left was a few red marks. She still had the bandage on her shoulder.

"What's the good news?" I asked her.

She pointed to the little table in the corner. Someone had set up a Christmas tree.

"The nurses did it," she said. "Wasn't that nice of them?"

"Yes."

Now that I was face to face with her, I had trouble telling her how I felt.

"They told me you stayed a long time to see how I was doing."

"Yeah, I guess I was kind of worried."

"You can say it."

"Say what?"

"That you love me."

"Okay, I love you."

"But do you mean it?"

"Yes," I said and bent over to kiss her.

"You two need to get a room." It was Ollie. "Oh, you already have one."

"Lee was just telling me how much he loves me."

"What a guy."

Ollie pecked Sheila on the forehead.

"How is the patient this morning?"

"Great. The nurses put a tree up for me and Lee loves me. How could it be better?"

Ollie looked at me. "I don't know. Be careful what you wish for."

Sheila laughed. It made me feel good to see her doing better.

Ollie took the journal out of his coat pocket.

"You feel up to listening to this?"

"What is it?"

"A journal that Mr. Edwin Barnett kept. His secretary thinks it made give us a lead."

"I didn't know she had that."

"We didn't either until yesterday. I picked it up this morning."

He fished a key out of his pants pocket.

"Who will do the honors?"

Sheila raised her hands.

He handed it to her.

"Unlock it and we'll see what it says."

She had to work the key to make it work, but finally got it.

"Who wants to read it?" I asked.

Sheila flipped through the book.

"Why don't you alternate dates?"

"How about you?"

"No thanks, I'll listen."

"Are you sure you're up to it?" Ollie asked her.

"Yes. I want to see what happens. If I doze off, keep going. I'll catch up later."

"Okay," Ollie said. "Who starts?"

"You," I said. "This is your case."

Ollie sat in the chair at the foot of Sheila's bed. I sat on the couch off to the side.

"And story time begins," he said opening it.

<u>Saturday, May 15th</u>: Neda is off on one her jaunts today. I don't know why she needs so much luggage just for a few days. I think she has a lover, but I don't have the desire to check on her. It's just not worth the trouble. I'm tired of her and I'm sure she's tired of me. I could divorce her, but mother would not approve. She would rather have an adulterous daughter-in-law than a divorced son. It would look bad on the company and the Barnett name. Maybe my lovely wife's plane will crash, or

her ship will sink. That may sound morbid, but I feel certain she feels the same way about me. If I dropped dead right now, she'd be a wealthy woman, but I think mother would try to block the insurance somehow. I don't know if she can legally do it, but she has enough influence to get anything she wants. She can be very persuasive when it suits her needs. I have to make a decision. I can't go on living like this.

Tuesday, May 18th: Neda came home today. She wouldn't tell me where she's been   I don't know why I bother. I'm tempted to slap her around some, but it wouldn't do any good. It would give her a reason for divorce and a large settlement. Mother would be furious if I did that, so I go on without any end in sight.

"It gets interesting right off the bat," I said.

"Edwin Barnett sounds wormy to me," Sheila said. "How could he run a large company?"

"I believe Momma Barnett was running things," Ollie said. "If this doesn't improve, I'd have to say he was only a figurehead doing mother's bidding."

Sheila yawned and closed her eyes.

"Don't stop on my account," she said.

Thursday, June 17th: Neda is scheduled to leave on another trip. This time she told me was going to Jamaica. I'm sure she has a lover. That being said I have made a decision. I decided to have an affair, maybe several while she is away. It must be discreet. It can't be anyone who has any ties to us or the company. I have decided on the working class. If I offer enough money, I will get a taker and buy silence. I went into a bank today, but not one where they know me by sight. The lobby was quiet and I went up to the window. Her name plate said she was Lavender Giles. I didn't see a wedding ring on her finger, so I assumed she was single. I gave her one my cards and asked to meet me at my office the next day. She wanted to know why. I told her I had a proposition for her and it could be worth $10,000 if she accepted. She told she would. I figured she could use the money because I know tellers don't make much. I felt her eyes on my back as I walked out.

"This guy's becoming scum already," I said.
"Money may not buy happiness," Ollie said, "but it can rent satisfaction for a while."

<u>Friday, June 18th</u>: I told Doreen I was expecting someone and she was to let her in without question and we were not to be disturbed. Lavender was apprehensive about meeting me. I told her I understood. I put an envelope on the desk and pushed it to her. I told her to open it. She gasped. Ten thousand dollars in twenty-dollar bills. I told her if she would spend one night with me, it was hers. No questions asked. If she didn't, she could walk out now, and no harm done. She thumbed through the bills in the envelope and agreed.

"Why such small bills?" Sheila said without opening her eyes.
"No one would think of tracing them," Ollie said. "Plus, it is easier to spend a twenty than trying to break hundred dollar bills all the time."
"At least he's thinking ahead," I said. "He's not leaving a trail of breadcrumbs."
Sheila opened her eyes and looked at me. "Breadcrumbs?"
"I remember Hansel and Gretel."
"Can we get on with it?" Ollie asked.
"Yes," Sheila said and put her head on the pillow and closed her eyes.

<u>Saturday, June 19th</u>: I met Lavender at the Seacoast Motel. I told her to check us in as Mr. and Mrs. Sam Bass after the Old West outlaw. I told her to get a room in the back. She did that and we went to the room. Needless to say I was nervous, but she appeared calm. Probably thinking about ten thousand tax free dollars. I will not go into the sordid details, but I will say it was a good night. She dressed early the next morning and left with her money. I laid there and thought it was pretty good. I could do this again the next time Neda leaves. That was my plan. I would have to wait and see if I could go through it once more.

<u>Friday, July 16th</u>: I'm sitting in the club lounge thinking about who to try next when she walked right up to me. Her name is Naomi Queen. She is a strikingly tall black woman with a vibrant personality. She is a waitress at the club. I know I said I wanted to stay away from those who know me, but I was taken with her. I asked her to sit down. We talked for a while and I made my offer. This time it was $20,000.

"Twenty?" I gasped.
"All it takes is money," Ollie said. "Shall I go on?"
I waved for him to continue.

She didn't bat an eye. She agreed. I told her to meet me at the Seacoast Motel the next night. She showed up at the appointed time, but with her husband.

I almost choked.
"Her husband?"
Sheila stirred in the bed but didn't wake up.
"Maybe she's into threesomes," Ollie said.
"Barnett has big balls," I said. "Going through with this with the husband there. Go on."

I was surprised, but she assured me nothing was wrong. His name is Alonzo. Not very tall, but muscular. We shook hands, which was strange for me. She told me they were swingers and this was nothing new to them, except the money. They usually did it for fun, not money. She went to check us in under the same names as before with the same location. And we got it. Alonzo left us to pick her up the next morning. She undressed me then I undressed her. We spent a wonderful night together. She did things I didn't think possible. The next morning Alonzo showed up. She took the money and left after kissing me on the lips. Another successful night.

A nurse came in to check Sheila's vitals. We watched quietly and waited. Ollie continued after she left.

<u>Friday, August 20th</u>: I was looking for something to read so I went to the local Books-A-Million. I don't know what I was looking for, just browsing. One of the salesladies came up to me and asked if she could be of service to me. I nodded and smiled. Her name tag said Peggy Rogers. She looked to be in her early thirties and cute. I made my pitch right there in the fiction section. She shook her head at first but mellowed some when I told her she could make $30,000.

"The ante keeps going up," I said. "How much money is this guy willing to spend?"

"It looks like the sky's the limit," Ollie said.

Sheila stirred and woke up.

"Anything good?"

Ollie and I looked at each other and smiled.

"What's so funny?"

"It appears Edwin Barnett is not the good little boy everyone thought," Ollie said.

"Just listen," I said, "it keeps getting better."

We sat in the coffee shop and I laid out the plan. I don't know if she was married, but by this time I didn't care. One thing I do know is money will override most common sense especially if you don't have it, money, not sense, although while I'm doing this, common sense doesn't enter into the equation. She looked around to see if anyone could hear us. They couldn't. They were in their own little world. Anyway, she agreed.

<u>Saturday, August 21st</u>: Peggy Rogers met me at the same motel. We went through the same routine, and surprisingly got the same room. She told me the desk clerk looked at her kind of funny. I shrugged it off. She had a nice body, but then something hit me. I watched her undress, but I saw Naomi Queen. She was the one I really wanted. I was in love with her.

"Here it comes," Sheila said. "The complications."
"Complications?" I asked.
"Yeah. He's in love with a black woman, no offense, Ollie."
"None taken," he said, "I am, too."
"I don't think Momma Barnett would approve," I said. "Plus, she's got a muscle head husband. I'm sure he wouldn't approve."
"Only if the money kept coming in," Ollie said. "May I?"
"Please do," I said.

I shook Naomi Queen from my mind, but it wasn't easy. Peggy was good and I enjoyed it. She wasn't in any hurry to leave the next morning, so we did it again. She said she had to go to work. I thanked her. She picked up the envelope without checking the contents and left.

"Thanked her?" Sheila exclaimed. "He thanked her? Did she serve him breakfast?"
"Apparently so," I said. "But apparently she served him more than breakfast."

"You know what I mean. You pay a woman thirty thousand dollars and then you thank her. The money would be thanks enough."

"The man has manners."

"He's got money and that's about it."

Ollie jumped between us.

"You two can discuss Edwin Barnett's manners after we finish the performance. I can't wait to see how this ends."

"I don't think it's going to be one of those 'they lived happily ever after' stories," Sheila said.

I sat there a while thinking about Naomi Queen. I even thought about calling her and offering more money, but I didn't know how Alonzo would react. I got dressed and went home.

"I'm thirsty," Ollie said. "How about a drink?"

"What do you have in mind?" Sheila asked.

"Coffee for me and you."

"Nothing for me," she said, "but you better get him something."

Ollie left the room and came back with coffee and a Diet Dr. Pepper.

"Would you like to read?" he asked handing me the can.

"No, go ahead. You're doing fine. I am mesmerized by your voice."

Sheila could only roll her eyes.

<u>Friday, September 17th</u>: I didn't feel like eating at the club or at home. Neda and I left at the same time without as much as a good-bye and hope you have a good trip. We acted like the other didn't exist. Just as well we didn't talk because it would have ended up in an argument. I had a thought the other day and it scared me. If I did press Neda on her excursions, she may file for divorce anyway. I don't think it would take much to push her to it. I went to a small mom and pop restaurant. It was a nice change of pace. Of course, I hit on the waitress. Her

name is Selma Wicks. She's in her forties, tall, and thin. She looked tired and aged beyond her real age. She took my order and I ate quietly. When she returned for the check, I gave her a nice tip and my card. She turned it over and gasped. I had written my proposal on the back with the tidy sum of $40,000.

I choked and spilled the drink in my lap.
"Forty grand?"
"That's what it says," Ollie said.
"I'm not surprised," Sheila said, "he probably thinks paying all the money will clear his conscious."
"There's no doubt the women he chose could use it," Ollie said.
I wiped my pants, but it left a wet spot until it dried.
"You might want to move faster next time," Sheila smiled. "And I wouldn't go out in public with your pants like that. People might get the wrong idea."
"I'm glad to see you're feeling better," I said tossing the napkin in the trash. "I'll keep that in mind."
"You entertain me. Please continue, Ollie.
I sat back down and sipped my drink.

She flipped the card over to the front. I could see she recognized my name. She sat down across from me. She wanted to know what it was about. I told her it was exactly like it said, but she didn't have to go through with it. She told me she could use the money. It was just her and her young son living with her mother. I asked about the father. She told me he died two years ago in an industrial accident. She got a settlement, but it wasn't much. She accepted.

<u>Saturday, September 18th</u>: We met at the motel. She sat in the car with me. I handed her the envelope with the money and told her to check it. Her hands shook as she thumbed through the bills. I told her it was not too late, but I knew she'd go through with it when she saw all that money. We went to the

same room. She was nervous which made me nervous, but we made it through the night. She thanked me in the morning because she needed the money. I thanked her for a lovely evening. She left about half an hour before me.

"At least he has manners," Sheila said. "Thanking each other like they'd just made a deal."

"They did have a deal," I said. "She has a product to sell and he has the money to buy it. Purely business.

"Ollie," Sheila said, "Please go on so he won't talk."

Ollie sipped his coffee and went on.

<u>Friday, October 15th</u>: I went to a convenience store to gas up my car and went in to get me something to drink. The clerk behind the counter was young but looked much older. She appeared to have a lot of unwelcomed miles on her face. Her name tag said Mabel. I felt sorry for her having to work who knows how many hours and not making much money. I struck up a conversation with her. She was shy. I had to pull the words out of her then I made her the proposition. She almost collapsed when I mentioned $50,000 but agreed because she needed the money. Sounds like a standard response. I guess they do it for the money and not for me.

Ollie waited for some remark from me or Sheila about the amount. We kept quiet. We could have figured how much it would jump.

<u>Saturday, October 16th</u>: I had another surprise waiting for me. When her car pulled up, I got out to meet her. Her husband was with her. He was big and looked mean. I didn't want to cross him and thought about calling it off. I didn't like the looks of him. He struck me as someone with a quick temper. He wanted to know about the money. He wasn't interested in what I would do with his wife. I explained the procedure. She

went in and got the key to the same room. He said he would be back in the morning to pick her up. I put the envelope with the money on the dresser. I told her to count it, but she said she trusted me. Imagine that. I'm basically preying on women who are broke and buying their services. They were prostitutes to me and I was an adulterer. And she's thanking me. Things didn't go so well. Like I said before I was in love with Naomi Queen or at the very least, I wanted her again. Mabel wanted to know what I wanted her to do. I told her take off her clothes. She did, but I didn't pay attention. She stood in front of me trembling. She was not attractive to me. Then she started crying. I decided I didn't want to go through with it. I told her to put her clothes back on. She cried the whole time which upset me, but I don't know why. I didn't care about her. She called her husband and things went downhill from there. He kicked the door in and wanted to know what the hell was going on. I told him. He wanted to know about the money. I told him no. He became angry and threatened to "beat my ass" and take the money. I told him to try if he could afford it. Mabel stood off to the side and cried. When he saw he wouldn't win he grabbed her arm and left, but not before he said this wasn't over. I shrugged it off and thought nothing of it. I spent the night there and went home in the morning. I decided I had enough of this. No more overnighters.

"There's no last name?" I asked.
"No," Ollie said. "Just Mabel."
"This guy gets worse with every woman," Sheila said. "I'll bet you have your murderer right there."
"The husband," I said.
"Right. All you have to do is prove it."
"I think we have a motive," Ollie said.
"Anymore?" I asked.
"Yes, one more entry."

<u>Wednesday, November 17th</u>: I'm supposed to meet him here tonight. He wanted to come late so we could be alone to discuss the situation. The situation in question is the money he feels I owe them from last month's cancelled "date", he called it. He feels I owe them the money because they went through with their part of the bargain. He said it wasn't their fault if I didn't want her. I told him since the deal wasn't consummated, I wasn't liable for payment. He became angry on the phone. I'm sitting here waiting for him to show. I'm nervous because I feel he will lose his temper and do me in. I hear the noise from a large truck. It must be him. I want to get this over with and forget I ever heard of Mabel Ramby.

"That's it," Ollie said. "He must have put it up when he heard the truck."

"Ramby," I said. "That name sounds familiar."

"The bar," Sheila said. "The guy with Philo Griggs was named Hastings Ramby. I remember because he gave me the creeps."

"Could be our guy," Ollie said.

I looked at Sheila.

"We have to talk about something."

Ollie stood and said, "I'll go down to the coffee shop. This has the makings of a disagreement."

"What is it?" she asked after Ollie left.

"Crystal said you could stay with her."

"I told you—"

"I know you told me, but I need to know you're safe until I figure out if Hastings Ramby is our killer. Come on, swallow your pride. She's offering and it will make me feel better."

She frowned but said nothing.

"Don't try to be a hero," I said. "It's just until you heal. For a few days."

I walked over to the bed and stroked her arm.

"Give it a try, an honest effort. Crystal will be at work most of the time. You can relax and heal then we'll get back to whatever's normal."

"Okay," she finally said. "But this is on your head."

"I accept the responsibility."

"This better work out, Lee, or I'll never forgive you."

"It will, I promise."

She grabbed me around the neck and kissed me.

"This better not take long. I'm ready to get back to work."

"It'll fly by, you'll see."

"Okay, I'll give it a try. It really would make me feel better not to be alone."

"Good. That's what I want to hear."

Ollie knocked on the door and came in.

"Everything okay?"

"Yeah, fine," I said. "Sheila will stay with Crystal for a while to recuperate."

"Good," he said.

The nurse came in with some good news. The doctor will release her the next day if she keeps improving.

"I'm not supposed to tell you that," she said to Sheila smiling.

"My lips are sealed."

She checked Sheila's vitals.

"Good," she said. "You look healthy as a horse. This your man?"

I blushed.

"That's him. Not much to look at, is he?"

The nurse looked me and down.

"I'd take him. Bye."

"Bye," Sheila said.

"I needed that," I said when the nurse left.

"You can take it."

Ollie smiled.

"I know you two will get married someday. You already act like you're married."

"We better go," I said. "I need to call Crystal."

I kissed her on the forehead. She pulled me down and kissed me on the lips.

"Thanks," she whispered.

"My pleasure."

"Come on, Cameron," Ollie said. "I'm getting sick to my stomach. I'm not accustomed to seeing you like this."

"Get used to it," Sheila said as we walked out.

13

Thursday, December 23rd

Sheila was dressed when I arrived at the hospital. The nurse was there helping her pack up her belongings and the tree.

"Ready to go?" I asked.

"Yes," Sheila said.

"She's good as new," the nurse said smiling.

"I'll try to keep her that way," I said. "Thanks for everything."

She waved off the remark.

"My pleasure. Every patient should be as good as your girlfriend."

She hugged Sheila and said, "Take care."

The nurse walked out as Crystal came in.

There was an awkward moment between them.

"You two might as well kiss and make up or whatever women do when they've been on the outs," I said. "Believe it not, you will have to talk to each other if you're living under the same roof. Understand how that works?"

"Yes, we know," Sheila said and put out her hand to Crystal.

"I guess I owe you an apology. It's been a long time."

"We can talk about it after you're settled," Crystal said. "Ready?"

On cue the nurse came in pushing a wheelchair.

"I can walk," Sheila said.

"I know you can, dear, but it's hospital policy. Enjoy it while you can."

She patted the seat.

Sheila sat down and held her Christmas tree. I carried the rest like the pack mule I was.

"Follow me," Crystal said to me. "I'm parked outside the door so Sheila can ride with me."

We rode down in silence. The nurse pushed Sheila up to Crystal's car and helped her in.

I retrieved my car and followed them.

I followed Crystal heading south. We passed some of the more upscale neighborhoods and turned left just past the mall. Her apartment turned out to be a townhouse.

"Living Room to your left," she said when we were standing in the hallway. "Kitchen straight ahead. Upstairs to your right is your bedroom. It's made up for you. You even have your own bath. To the left is my room."

"Do you have a bath?" I asked.

"Yes," she smiled. "This is luxury."

It looked like it to me. I didn't know what reporters made, but the place looked comfortable. Maybe I should change professions.

"I'll carry her stuff upstairs," I said taking the tree.

Sheila looked around.

"Maybe we could put the tree down here."

"Fine with me," Crystal said.

She cleared a small table in the center of the room then pushed it against a corner window.

"There. We can turn on the lights."

I knew Sheila was wondering why Crystal didn't have her own tree, but she let it go…at least while I was there.

Sheila, holding her shoulder, went ahead of me up the stairs. The going was slow, but we made it. I hauled her belongings and put them on the bed.

She sat on the edge. I could see she was tired.

"Why don't you lie down," Crystal suggested. "Rest up."

"Thanks, I will," Sheila said and lay back.

Crystal took her things and put them away then we went downstairs.

"She'll be okay," Crystal said.

"Thanks for doing this. I know she didn't give you any reason to."

"We'll be fine. Check on her whenever you like." She looked at me frowning. "Something wrong?"

"No, nothing's wrong, but I have an idea."

"Run it by me."

"Do you need someone else here with you…for protection I mean?"

"No, I don't think so. Who did you have in mind?"

"I'd like to talk to Philo Griggs and see if he can keep an eye on you two."

"Why him?"

"We talked to him. I don't think he's a bad guy. Okay, he screwed up and got caught. I don't think he's involved with Barnett's murder. I'd put my money on Kruger before Griggs. It's up to you. He could probably use the company…and…after all, it is Christmas."

"What if he is on it? What would you do if he does something to us like kill us? How would you feel?"

"Not very good, I'm sure."

Crystal walked around the room and looked at Sheila's little tree.

"You want to know why I don't have a Christmas tree?" she said without turning around.

"I was wondering, but that's your business."

She turned to me.

"Well, for one thing, my father died on Christmas. I was fifteen. Ever since then, I dreaded the holidays. I've adjusted to it but can't bring myself to put up a tree."

"We all celebrate Christmas in our own way," I said feeling philosophical. "I don't put one up simply because I don't want to go through the trouble."

"But Sheila likes Christmas."

"Oh, yes. She's gets excited the closer it gets."

"Anyway, that has nothing to do with what we were talking about."

"You have your reasons for telling me."

I picked at one of the small bulbs on the tree.

"I can tell you one thing, though. If you let her, Sheila will get you in the Christmas spirit."

"It may be what I need," she said. "Maybe we can help each other heal."

"Give it a try. If doesn't work, it doesn't work."

"If she's up to it."

"What about Griggs?"

"Tell you what. You talk to him. If you're comfortable with what you find out, I'll go along. It may be nice having a man around the house."

"Don't get attached. I don't believe he's your type."

"I don't have a type. If they walk upright and can speak the King's English, they have a foot in the door."

I smiled.

"Okay, I'll go talk to him and let you know."

She handed me a business card with her cell phone number on the back.

"Watch yourself, Lee."

"Yeah, I do, but it isn't working out so well."

"You and Sheila will be fine."

I nodded and left.

I went by Ollie's office to touch base. He got in touch with Mabel Ramby for us to go to talk to her the next morning, Christmas Eve.

"We need to speak with her about this journal," he said.

"She may know something about her part," I said, "but I doubt if she knows about the others. I'll bet she doesn't know they got paid and I'll bet none know about the others."

"Probably. I also want to speak with the Barnett women about this."

"You mean show them the journal."

"Yes," he said patting his jacket pocket.

"That's good. I want to see their reaction. Yvonne Barnett will have a cow when she reads that. That will definitely give the family a black eye. Did you tell Jack about the journal?"

Ollie shook his head. "No. Let's be honest here. If I show it to him, he'll want it. I want to speak with Mabel Ramby and the Barnetts before I turn it over to him."

"Then it goes into the evidence room."

Ollie nodded.

"And things can disappear from there. With Yvonne Barnett's money she can make the whole room disappear."

"Okay by me," I said heading for the door. "What time for Mabel Ramby?"

"Meet me here around eight-thirty. We can go in my car."

"I don't think she'll mention it to her husband. I'm willing to bet she's afraid of him."

"I'm glad you don't put any money on all those bets you're offering."

I got to the Eight Ball Lounge around five. As an afterthought I called Xavier Unger and asked him to meet me there. I explained what I wanted to do. He agreed.

Philo was sitting at the bar talking to the bartender. I climbed on a stool beside him. He looked at me and smiled. Xavier came in and sat on the other side of him. Philo didn't smile when he saw him.

His head swiveled back and forth between us.

"What did I do? I didn't do nothing."

"Take it easy," Xavier said. "We are just here to speak with you."

"What about?"

Xavier looked around the joint.

"Why don't we go to one of those booths."

Philo picked up his beer then thought better of it.

"Take it," Xavier said.

He sat across from us.

"Just got off work. I'm bushed."

He looked it, too. His clothes were dirty and sweaty.

"How are things going, Philo?" Xavier asked.

"Good, Mr. Unger. I'm staying out of trouble."

"Good, good. Mr. Cameron has something he'd like to ask you."

I had the floor.

"You told me you didn't have anything to do with Edwin Barnett's murder."

"That's right."

"Are you willing to swear to it at the risk of going back to prison?"

He didn't hesitate.

"I would."

"Do you know anything about Barnett's murder?"

"Only what I hear on the news and read in the paper. I'm staying away from that mess."

"Good. I have a proposition for you."

"What?"

"Mr. Unger has assured me you're safe and he agrees with my plan."

Philo sipped his beer but didn't say anything. He did glance at his parole officer.

"My secretary, Sheila. Remember her?"

"Yes."

"Did you know she got shot?"

He nodded.

"Too bad."

"We believe the same person who shot her killed Edwin Barnett. The slugs came from the same rifle. She's staying with a friend until she can get back on her feet."

He nodded again.

"What I'd like you to do is stay with Sheila and her friend for a couple of days. I spoke with the friend about it and the friend agrees. It would only be for a few days."

"What about my job? If I'm gone too long, I could lose it. I can't afford to lose it."

"I've spoken with Mr. Quint," Xavier said. "And he agreed. He really didn't have much choice when I told him it would help catch the killer and I would go through the courts if necessary. Your job will be waiting for you when you get back."

"I don't know," Philo said. "I'm trying to stay out of trouble."

"Look, Philo," I said. "There shouldn't be any trouble. You'll just be there with these two women as security. If you have to do something to protect them, even if it means using force, we're behind you, but you have to be careful."

"I've touched base with the judge that sent you to prison," Xavier said. "I told him what is going on."

"Besides," I said, "if he doesn't go along, Yvonne Barnett will flaunt her money and make him do whatever we want."

Philo shook his head.

"Must be good to have money."

"I wouldn't know. I work for a living just like you."

"How about it?" Xavier asked.

"What if I don't want to?"

"You walk away and drink your beer like nothing happened. You're not obligated."

"But it would help. Right?"

"It would make me feel better," I said, "and those two defenseless women would feel safer."

What I knew, but Philo obviously didn't, was those two women were nowhere near defenseless.

"Okay, Mr. Cameron. Mr. Unger. I'll do it, but you're sure I'll still have my job."

"I swear it," I said. "I'll make sure you do."

He put out his hand to us and we shook it.

"When can you go?" I asked.

"How long do you want me to plan for?"

"We'll play it by ear. Let's look at least until Monday."

"Did you have plans for Christmas?" Xavier asked him.

He shook his head.

"I think I was scheduled to work, but no, nothing."

"See," I said, "you get to spend Christmas with two women."

He smiled.

"Been a long time since I had a real Christmas."

"This will be real," I said.

I felt better when we left.

We knocked on Crystal's door around six-thirty. Sheila answered.

She hugged me and looked at Philo.

"You mind if we come in?" I asked her.

She opened the door wide because Philo filled it.

"Come in," Crystal said, "and sit down."

She was sitting at the dining room table.

"Crystal told me what you have in mind," Sheila said.

"Were you against it?" I asked.

"At first, but she talked me into it."

She looked at Philo.

"How do you feel about this?"

"Nervous."

"So am I. Mr. Cameron thinks he can run our lives."

"I'm trying to protect you."

"I appreciate it."

"Mr. Griggs—," Crystal started.

"Philo."

"Philo, if it's okay with you, you can sleep on the couch down here."

He looked in the direction she was pointing and nodded.

"Okay with me."

"My home is your home," she said. "If Lee here trusts, you so do I."

"Thanks."

"One more thing," I said. "It might a good idea to let Philo answer the door."

"I don't have many visitors," Crystal said.

"He can screen whoever wants in."

"That okay with you?" Crystal asked him.

"Sure."

"Good," I said rising. "I'll check on everyone tomorrow, but it'll probably be in the evening. Ollie and I have a couple of people to see."

Sheila walked me to the door. Crystal talked to Philo to give us some privacy.

"Hold it," Philo said. "I want to thank you for trusting me. Not many people do."

"No problem," I said shaking his hand.

But that wasn't good enough for him. He grabbed me in a bear hug and lifted me off the floor.

"You can depend on me," he said.

"Good," I said when he put me down trying to catch my breath.

"I didn't hurt you, did I?"

"No, just my pride."

I waved at Crystal, shook Philo's hand, kissed Sheila a good one, and left.

14
Friday, December 24th

Christmas Eve. It wasn't the way we had planned on spending it. Sheila's doing fine and getting along well with Philo and Crystal. I'll go over tonight. I guess we'll do a little celebrating. I don't know if Sheila's up to it. I'm betting she is. Since she love's the season so much, I can't picture her not doing something. I've never seen her feel sorry for herself. No need to start now.

Ollie and I are on our way to see Mabel Ramby. When he called her, he told her about the journal. That was how we found out about her. With any luck, Hastings will be there, but I'm not putting my money on that horse.

The Rambys live in a mobile home park north of town. It's across from the North Ridge Shopping Center. The area is divided by a four-lane highway heading out of town. The park, North Ridge Mobile Home Park, is a nice one. I've been through there before. It's kept clean and neat unlike most parks. Those are trailer parks to me. The nice ones are mobile home parks, but that's another story.

Ollie went in to get the lot number. It was located across from the office. A swimming pool separated the two. We walked.

There was an old car parked under the carport. Everything looked as it should be. If nothing else, the Rambys were neat and tidy. There were tracks on the concrete slab alongside the driveway where a heavy truck would normally be parked. That was for Hastings' dually, I'm sure.

Mabel was expecting us and opened the door before we could knock.

"Come in," she said.

Her house was spotless. I don't know if she kept it like that all the time or it was for our benefit. She was dressed in a worn house dress with slippers.

She led us to the kitchen table where she set down three coffee mugs then filled them. I like the aroma of coffee, but don't drink it. I sipped a little to make it look nice. Ollie looked at me and shook his head.

"Thanks for seeing us, Mrs. Ramby," Ollie said.

He appeared to be enjoying his brew.

"I knew the police would eventually come calling."

"Why is that?"

"Hastings' been acting funny ever since…you know."

"How?"

"He's been mad since that night. He said that Mr. Barnett owed us money and he wanted it."

"What is your opinion?" I asked her, starting to enjoy the coffee.

She shrugged.

"I told him to let it go. What's done is done. No good can come out of him pushing that man for the money."

Ollie took out the journal and put in on the table.

Mabel looked at it.

"This is the journal I told you about," Ollie said.

He pushed it to her.

"Mr. Barnett was having flings, if you will, with a number of women. You were the last according to what he wrote."

"But…but I…"

"I know," I said, "you didn't do anything, but he felt it was necessary to write about it."

Ollie handed it to her.

"Read this," he said. "My partner and I will sit in the living room to give you some privacy."

Ollie sat in a love seat that made him sink in.

"Soft?" I said smiling.

He just nodded and tried to lift himself up a little.

"No way," he said. "I'll just wait until I am ready to get up."

I sat in a straight back chair facing the front window.

Mabel Ramby was an excellent housekeeper from the looks of things. Everything appeared to be where it belonged. And clean.

"This woman probable deserves someone better than what she has," Ollie said.

"I agree, but we have choices. Apparently, she chooses to stay with him."

"Maybe she doesn't have a choice. You know, no money, no job skills. She needs his income to live."

"That may be the case," I said looking out the window.

"You think he'll show?"

"That would be our good luck," I said. "I've been watching the window. If he pulls up, I'll see him."

"Glad we parked at the office. He won't know anyone is here."

I looked toward the kitchen. All was quiet.

"She's taking it well," Ollie said.

Then we heard her crying and went to meet her.

"I know it's not good to relive your experience," Ollie said. "But we need to know if you know any of the other women."

She shook her head and wiped her face with a washcloth.

Ollie put the journal back in his coat pocket.

"Mrs. Ramby," Ollie said, "you said your husband was upset because Mr. Barnett didn't pay you."

"That's right."

"And he's been upset ever since?"

"Yes."

"Did he say anything about trying to collect it?"

"He talked on and on about going to see Mr. Barnett, but I don't know if he ever did."

Ollie and I looked at each other.

"Does your husband own a rifle?" I asked.

"Yes, he likes to hunt."

"Like what?"

"Deer. He won't hunt anything else. He said he likes shooting from a far off. He said it's more sporting like that."

"You ever go with him."

She shook her head.

"No, he said huntins not for women. It's a man's sport."

"Do you argue with your husband?"

"No, he won't allow that neither. He likes to make the decisions about everything."

"He ever hit you?" Ollie asked.

"Some, but not hard."

"Mrs. Ramby," I said, "do you think Hastings killed Edwin Barnett?"

"OH! NO!" she said getting up and pouring us more coffee. "He wouldn't do that."

"What makes you so sure?"

"He's rough and all that and he knocks me around some. He didn't want me to do that with Mr. Barnett until he heard how much he was goin to pay me."

"After he heard, he was all right with it?"

"Yes," she said bowing her head. "He said we can use the money. It was moren I ever seen."

"What does your husband like to do," Ollie asked, "when he's not working or hunting?"

"He plays pool a lot."

"For money?"

She shrugged.

"If he does, he don't give me none. I don't know."

"Do you know Philo Griggs?"

"Only when he talks about him. He's plays pool with Hastings. At least that's what he told me."

Ollie handed Mabel Ramby his card.

"If you think of anything, please call me."

We stood to leave.

"Does your husband know you spoke with us today?"

"No. If he knew that he'd be mad for sure."

"Let's keep it that way for the time being."

She walked us to the door and out on the deck.

"Do you think Hastings killed Mr. Barnett?"

"We're just checking people out," Ollie said. "We don't have any suspects yet. We're just gathering information."

She walked to the end of the drive and watched our car until we were out of sight. She looked like one scared woman.

We were on our way in when Ollie's cell phone rang.

"Yes…okay…we're on our way…bye."

"The Barnett ladies just got to my office."

"Oh, boy," I said, "neither one will be too happy about waiting."

"I suppose not," he said, "and they won't be too happy about their husband and son."

Yvonne Barnett was seated across from Ollie's desk. Neda stood at the window.

Ollie sat at his desk. I stood in one corner.

"Mrs. Barnett, Neda," he said, "please have a seat."

Neda glared at me and sat.

"I hope you have a good reason for calling us here," Neda said.

"Quiet, Neda," Yvonne said. "I'm sure Officer Fletcher has a good reason to want to talk to us."

She puffed up but didn't say anything.

Ollie got things rolling.

"Did you know your husband, and your, son was having affairs?"

"Nonsense!" Neda said.

"I find that rather hard to believe," Yvonne said.

"Would you recognize his handwriting?"

They nodded.

He took the journal out of his pocket and handed it to Yvonne. We didn't give them the same courtesy we gave Mabel Ramby.

"What's this?" Neda asked.

"It's a record of your husband's whereabouts for the last six months."

Yvonne thumbed through it then handed it to Neda.

"Is that his handwriting?" Ollie asked.

"Yes," Yvonne answered.

"It's hard to tell," Neda said.

"It's his," Yvonne said. "What about it?"

"Read it," Ollie said, "both of you. Read if from beginning to end then we'll discuss it."

They hesitated.

"We'll sit here until you do," Ollie said, "if it takes all night. I want you to know what Mr. Barnett was up to."

They read. We waited. They're expressions went from surprised to anger to wonder. Yvonne closed the book.

"What do you think?" Ollie asked.

"It's a lie," Neda said.

"Is that his handwriting?"

"Yes, it looks like it."

"Then how can you say it's a lie. Why would he make all that up?"

"I don't know, but I can tell you it's a lie."

"Yvonne?" Ollie said.

"I'm not surprised," she said glaring at her daughter-in-law. "You're always globetrotting off instead of staying home and taking care of business."

"How was I to know?"

Yvonne held up the journal.

"Now you do."

She handed the journal to Ollie. He put it in his pocket.

Neda started to get up.

"Sit down," I said.

She hesitated then did.

"What happens now?" Yvonne said.

"We wanted you to see this," I said. "Remember what you told Jack about mudding the Barnett name? Well, you have it here."

"You can't publicize this," Yvonne said.

"This could be evidence," Ollie said. "We'll keep it quiet if we can, but I don't make promises I don't intend to keep."

"Who else knows about this?"

"Other than the women in the journal just the four of us plus my secretary," I said.

"Can she be trusted to keep her mouth shut?"

"She has no reason to talk about it."

Yvonne held out her hand.

"Give it to me."

"Why?"

"So, it can get buried. No one has to know."

I came around and stood by the side of the desk.

"Mrs. Barnett, the bullet that wounded my secretary, Sheila Arceneaux, in case you forgot her name, came from the same rifle that killed your son. What's written in here could be evidence when we find the killer. You can't have it."

She stiffened. She was not the same charming lady I had spoken with earlier.

"Officer Fletcher, I donate a lot of money to many campaigns. The people in those positions can have serious effects on your job and your career. If you give me that book, we'll go on like we were. You hunt for the killer."

"Mrs. Barnett," I said, "the same guy who shot your son shot my secretary. It has become personal with me. Your daughter-in-law fired me. That's okay. I mean to find the killer with or without your help and I don't give a damn if it bloodies the Barnett name. It's vengeance now for me and I'm not giving up anything that will help me find the killer. Understand?"

"You have no right to speak to me like that."

"You don't deserve any better. You're more concerned about your family name than who killed your son. Oh, you want the killer found, but it has to be on your conditions. Things don't work like that. I'm sure the killer won't care if your good name is tarnished."

I went to the window and looked out. I had to cool off.

"Does Crystal Hudson know about this?" Neda asked.

"No," Ollie said.

"But I can give it to her," I said without turning around.

I could hear the strain in her voice.

"You wouldn't dare."

"I would. She's just waiting for a good story."

"Hold it, everyone," Ollie said, "Let's not argue."

I turned around.

"What would your company's business partners say about this not to mention your customers? How would they take it? Would they bail out on you? Do your accountants juggle your books like you want us to juggle evidence?"

"Of course not," Yvonne answered.

"Then why do we need to do something illegal to please you. I'm not willing to go to jail for you."

I turned back to the window.

"Can we go now?" Neda asked.

"Shut up, Neda," Yvonne said.

She did.

"What do you want?" Yvonne asked.

Ollie held up the journal.

"We hold on to this. We'll try to convict the case without it, but if we need it to get that conviction, we use it. That's the best I can do."

"I want it when you're done."

"If we don't need it, I'll give it to you to do what you will."

"And I'll tell you why," I said turning around.

They turned to me. Yvonne was curious. Neda just wanted to get out.

"If this gets out, your business will suffer. Do you agree?"

"Yes, "Yvonne said.

"We don't know how much, but it will suffer. That affects everyone in town. If your business suffers, it trickles down. Maybe you care about that. Maybe you don't, but it'll happen. People may lose their jobs. The economy of the area will suffer. That's the impact your company has on this town not to mention the money you dump on politicians."

I moved closer to them.

"But you know what? I don't care about any of it if we can't catch the killer. He tried to kill me but was no good at it and shot Sheila. That pissed me off and I will catch that son-of-a-bitch."

I turned before anyone could say anything and left, slamming the door.

15

Monday, December 27th

The four of us spent Christmas together. Against her better judgment, Crystal let me stay the night with Sheila. We didn't bother to get the gifts, or whatever Sheila had under her tree in the office. Philo and Sheila shared their lives. Come to find out, they weren't that different. Both had lives less than ideal and had gotten into some binds they could have avoided had they thought ahead.

I was in Ollie's office discussing what to do next. The journal shed some light on the investigation, but we had to find Hastings Ramby and talk to him. He was our prime suspect, but we needed proof. I figured we were on the right track this time.

The call came around nine while we were brainstorming.

"Yes," Ollie said then looked at me.

I straightened up.

"What's wrong?"

"Yes. I'll tell him."

"Come on," he said grabbing his jacket. "We'll take my car."

He put on his siren and blue light and sped to Crystal's apartment.

"All I know right now is Hastings Ramby showed at Crystal's apartment. He shot Philo and Sheila. Uriah's there now."

I was out of Ollie's car before it slowed down. The place was covered in police cars and ambulances.

Ollie caught up with me and showed his ID to the officer standing outside the door.

When I went in, I saw Sheila lying at the foot of the stairs in an awkward position, but I didn't see any blood. Philo was on his back on the living floor. His chest was red. Crystal sat at the table with the Greenwood Parish coroner.

I went to Sheila.

"Don't touch her," Ollie said.

I looked at him and started to bend down.

"Don't do it, son," Uriah said.

Uriah Klug had been coroner for the last twenty years. He looked more like a mad scientist than a doctor. His hair stuck up like he put his finger in a light socket.

"I know she's a friend," he continued, "but this is a crime scene."

I fell to my knees. I couldn't keep from looking at her. I wanted to touch her, to kiss her, to tell her everything is going to be alright.

Uriah pushed a chair out for me. I struggled to my feet. I thought my legs would give out. Ollie helped me to the chair.

Crystal was crying.

"I…I…I'm sorry, Lee," she said between sobs.

I could only shake my head.

Ollie sat next to me.

"Uriah," he said.

"Oliver."

"Can you tell us what happened?" Ollie asked taking out his pad.

"I gave Miss Hudson something to calm her down," Uriah said. "I'll relate to you what she told me.

He opened his own little pad.

"It seems this fellow Hastings Ramby came by sometime between eight and eight-thirty. Philo Griggs opened the door, but wouldn't let him in. Miss Arceneaux was upstairs in her room. Miss Hudson was in the kitchen.

"Miss Hudson heard what was going on and stuck her head around the corner to see just enough where they couldn't see her. She heard Griggs call Ramby by name. Griggs forced Ramby back out and closed the door. Miss Hudson started to come out when the front door flew open.

"Ramby had a rifle. He held it against Griggs' stomach backing him up to where you see him now. That's when Ramby said he wanted to talk to Miss Arceneaux. Griggs' told him no and tried to grab the rifle. Ramby fired hitting him in the chest.

"It seems at this time Miss Arceneaux heard what was going on and came out to see. Ramby looked up and saw her. He turned and fired but missed. Apparently, the noise from the gun startled her.

She tried to jump back and lost her footing. She fell down the stairs and landed as you see her."

He pointed at Sheila.

"The police dug the slug out of the wall—"

He pointed up stairs.

"—at the top of the landing where Miss Arceneaux was standing.

"Ramby ran off. If he would have seen Miss Hudson, I'm sure he would have done her in, too. She's your witness, Oliver."

I didn't say anything. I was too stunned to talk. I could barely think and I wasn't so sure I was doing a very good job of that.

"Did Ramby say why he wanted to talk to Miss Arceneaux?"

"No," Crystal said shaking her head.

"How did Sheila die?" I asked.

"Broke her neck when she landed at the bottom. She has one arm broken, too. Looks like she tried to break her fall."

He put his arm on my shoulder.

"I'm sorry, son," he said, "Miss Hudson told me you and Miss Arceneaux were close friends."

"I loved her," I said. "No, I love her."

"When you're finished with your work here," Uriah said to Ollie, "I can take them. In the meantime, if you have any questions, I'll be outside."

"Thanks," Ollie said.

Uriah Klug shuffled out.

Sheila and Philo were surrounded by people with cameras maneuvering to get the right angles. It seemed like a gory job to me, but like they say, someone has to do it.

Finally, they put both in body bags and lifted them onto gurneys.

"I'll have an officer stay with you," Ollie told Crystal. "He probably wouldn't be dumb enough to come back, but you never know."

She thanked him and we left.

"This guy's probably desperate," Ollie said when we were on the way back to the office.

I was numb and couldn't rationalize.

"If he killed Barnett and shot Sheila at your office. Now he kills Philo Griggs and Sheila. No one knows what he'll do now. HE probably doesn't know what he'll do."

We went to Jack Vincent's office. Ursula was there.

"We're sorry for your—"

"Save it, Madam District Attorney," I said.

I often wondered how I would act if something like this happened. Now I knew. My emotions were in a battle. I was hurt and shocked, but I was mad as hell and I wanted to do something.

"I don't need your political bullshit," I said. "My best friend is lying in the morgue and I'm going to get who's responsible."

"I only meant to give you my condolences."

"That's nice, but not necessary. I know you feel that is what you have to say. I don't need it."

"Look, folks," Jack said, "let's not get into this again. We have work to do."

Ursula sat on the couch. Ollie stood. I paced.

"I don't think he'll go back home," Ollie said. "I'm sure by now his wife told him we were there to talk to her. Hell, he'll probably kill her."

"You think he would?" Ursula asked.

"What would he have to lose," Jack said. "He's killed two today and probably killed Edwin Barnett. What's one more? What could we do to him?"

"He may be at that bar where he hangs out," Ollie said.

"Why would he go there?" Jack asked.

"I don't know. Maybe he needs a drink. From what I understand, he goes there a lot. He may feel safe, but I don't know. He knows we'll be looking for him. My guess he would leave town."

"Give me his home address," Jack said picking up the phone. "What does he drive?"

Ollie gave him the address. I gave him the description of the truck.

"I'm going to send a car out there to see if the wife is okay and see if the truck's there."

We waited. I paced. No one said anything. Then Jack's phone rang.

"Yes…yes…thanks."

"The wife is there. She's pretty shook up. Other than that, she's all right. The truck is not there. The wife doesn't know where he is. It looked like she'd been packing, probably about to get away from him. The officer will stay there to make sure she's okay and will let us know if he shows up."

"Come on," I said to Ollie standing.

"Where to?"

"The Eight Ball Lounge. If he's there, I want him."

Ursula stood up.

"Detective Fletcher will make the arrest," she said. "We don't want to lose him because you broke some law to satisfy your need for revenge. You don't have the authority to arrest anyone."

I took a step toward her, but Ollie stopped me.

"Come on, Cameron," he said turning me around.

One day I'll have a real run in with her.

Ollie drove. I fumed.

I could see two other patrol cars parked down the road from the bar. Ramby's truck wasn't out front. I didn't expect it to be. I gave him credit for having some sense to try and hide it.

The radio went off and Ollie picked up the mic.

"The white dually is around back," the officer said. "It looks like he was trying to hide it, but it's hard to hide something that big."

"Right," Ollie said, "Thanks."

He hung up the mic.

"I can't believe our luck," I said. "I can't believe he's not heading for parts unknown. I can't believe he's that stupid. He has to know we'll check here."

"We don't have him yet."

Ollie parked in front and we got out. The two uniforms met us.

"Go around back and watch that door," he told one of the officers. "I don't want him reaching that truck."

The officer left then Ollie turned to the other.

"I'll make the arrest. You watch the front."

"I'm going with you," I said.

Ollie took me by my shoulders.

"Look, Cameron," he said. "I'm not telling you this as a cop, but as a friend. Let me handle it. You're not in the right frame of mind. We don't want this to get out of hand. If anything happens that looks illegal, his lawyer will get him off and then he disappears."

He turned to the officer.

"You come with me."

Then back to me.

"You watch the front door. There are no side doors so we should have all the exits covered."

He waited for me to answer, but I didn't. I wanted a piece of Ramby, but I understood what he was talking about. The law would have to handle it.

They started in then Ollie turned to me.

"If he gets away from us and comes out the front do what you will, but I didn't tell you that."

I nodded. They went in.

It seemed like forever waiting for them to come out. I hoped Ramby would get away and come out to meet me. I paced and looked at my watch…over and over.

But it didn't happen that way.

Ollie and the officer came out with Ramby in handcuffs. Blood ran down his face from a cut on his forehead.

"What happened?" I asked.

"He broke a beer bottle and came at us," Ollie said. "The officer laid him out with his weapon. I guess he thought his size would give him an advantage. Like you said, I can't believe he's that stupid."

"I'll sue you!" Ramby hollered. "I'll have your jobs!"

Then I forgot, or more likely ignored, everything everyone told me.

"I thought you said you didn't miss!" I yelled at him.

I punched him as hard as I could in the jaw. To my surprise he went down. I took him for tougher stock. I straddled his chest working over his face. I was like a crazy man.

Images of Sheila falling down the stairs kept coming to me. I see her trying to put out her arm to save herself. Hitting the landing with such force, it broke her neck. Did she think about me? Did she love me? Questions and images invade my mind.

Tears streaming down my cheek. I wanted to kill him. I meant to kill him. Justice be damned. To Hell with revenge being served cold. I was having my moment and didn't want to stop.

Ollie told me later that when the two uniforms pulled me off, I was growling like a rabid dog. That pretty much summed it up.

Ollie got me under control while the other two put Ramby in back of one of the cruisers.

"Why don't you go home?" Ollie said wiping me off then straightening his suit. "Get some rest. I know that's easy to say, but you need it. We'll take care of this bird."

I picked up my car but didn't go to my apartment. I wanted to talk to Crystal.

The officer let me in. She was sitting in the same spot where we left her.

When she saw me, she got up and hugged me.

"You want something to drink?" she asked. "I could fix some coffee or something."

"No, that's okay. Sit down."

I could see blood stains where Philo had lain.

"Did you get him?" she asked. "Did you kill the son of a bitch?"

"Yes, we got him, or Ollie and the officers got him. He's under arrest."

She got up and retrieved a box of tissue. Her eyes were red and swollen. I believe mine were, too.

"It's not your fault, Crystal. He must have followed one of us here. That's the only way he'd know where you lived."

"I'm in the book. I'm not that hard to find. He'd only have to know she was here."

"My bet is he followed us here. He's probably been watching us all along."

"That's scary."

"People like Hastings Ramby are scary…and dangerous."

"What will happen to him?"

"They'll interrogate him. He'll be charged with Philo's death and probably with Sheila's."

I stopped and wiped my eyes.

"They'll probably arrest me, too."

"Why?"

"When they brought him out of the bar, he was in handcuffs. I lost control and jumped on him. I meant to kill him. I beat him until the two officers pulled me off."

She smiled. "I know I shouldn't smile, but I can't have any sympathy with people like that. You got one in for the little people."

"I guess so, but I don't feel any better."

She reached over and took my hand.

"You may never feel better. The memories will be harsh and rear its ugly head now and then, but you'll get through it."

I nodded.

"Hopefully he'll confess to Edwin Barnett's murder. The slugs from Barnett and Sheila match his rifle.

She nodded like she understood.

"Did Dr. Klug leave anything out of what he told me happened here?"

"No, I don't think so."

"Ramby didn't say why he wanted to talk to Sheila?"

"No."

"I don't think he wanted to talk to her."

"Why would he ask?"

"I think he wanted to kill her. When she came out of her room at the top of the stairs, he had his opportunity, but he missed."

"Philo went for the gun."

"He gave up his life to save hers and it didn't work."

"He was a good guy. I know that now. He might have had some problems in the past, but I believe he was basically a good guy."

"I didn't think he was the killer when we talked to him."

"I might question his choice of friends."

"I guess I better go," I said. "Will you be okay?"

"Yes, I'll be fine. I'll go back to work tomorrow."

She walked me to the door.

"Can you tell the officer he can go since you caught him?"

"I'll get in touch with Ollie. They have to call him."

"Thanks," she said.

"No. Thank you."

I gave her a hug and left.

But I didn't go to my apartment. I went to Sheila's and as luck would have it, I found a parking spot by her apartment. What timing.

I let myself in and looked around. I took in her aroma. I should never forget it. I went out to the balcony and sat down. The children were down in the yard playing and screaming. I'm sure they were comparing Christmas gifts. That's what we did when I was a kid.

I closed my eyes and pictured her as I knew her. Try as I might, I couldn't get that last image out of my mind. It will take me a while to wipe that clean if ever. Maybe I shouldn't forget it. Maybe I should be reminded of what real love was as I knew it. Maybe she's up there shaking a finger at me because I didn't commit to her earlier. Maybe I shouldn't have let her in on this investigation. I told her it could be dangerous. She found out in the harshest way.

I don't know how long I sat there trying to remember as much as I could about her. I wondered why the two guys who mistreated her did what they did. She didn't deserve it. As far as I was concerned, she was a good woman.

It was dark when I left her apartment. I took one last look around. I didn't expect to be coming back. I opened the door, looked around, turned out the light, and closed and locked the door.

I cried all the way back to my place.

16

Wednesday, December 29th

As luck would have it, we had rain the night before. It had slacked off by morning, but it continued to be a steady drizzle throughout the day. I went to the office early. I couldn't sleep. I don't know why I'm here because my mind is not on anything. Hastings Ramby killed Philo Griggs and indirectly killed Sheila. It's almost a hundred percent he killed Edwin Barnett, but Ollie will have to work on that to prove it. I feel my job is done concerning Edwin Barnett.

I sipped my Diet DP while looking out the window. There was no crowd rushing around for Christmas. There was no kid with his foot on the wall of the building waiting for granny to show up and kick his ass. Only an empty street covered in a mist. The weather mirrored my mood. I turned occasionally expecting Sheila to walk in here unannounced with her acid tongue. No such luck. Not anymore. Not ever again.

Philo Griggs was buried by the parish. No one showed up to claim the body. I feel bad for him. He was a hero in my book. He did as I asked and died for it. So sad.

Crystal gave Philo and Sheila a good write up. She may see that as her way of sending them off in a blaze of glory.

Sheila's funeral is this morning. I'm not looking forward to it. How will I hold up? Tom and Ollie are supporting me emotionally. They are good friends.

The Christmas tree is still up in Sheila's office along with all her other decorations. I'm not in the mood to take them down yet. I may never be. I may leave them and just walk out and never come back.

I finished my drink and tossed the bottle at the can across the room. Perfect. It never touched the side. Sheila needed to see it. I knew I could do it.

"You see that?" I said looking at the ceiling.

I looked at my watch. It hadn't stopped. As they say, "time marches on." I could smash my watch and stop it, but that wouldn't really stop it. Nothing stops time.

It was time to go.

Baltimore Funeral Home was just around the corner, so I didn't get any real hurry to get there. I pulled my car around back out of the way.

Sheila was in one of the state rooms. She wouldn't have the type of funeral reserved for the likes of Edwin Barnett. But that would be all right with her. It was all right with me.

The room was empty when I got there except for the director and his helper putting out the flowers. When they finished, I went up and looked at her. And that's all I could do was look. I was still having a hard time dealing with her death. She was too young. She needed to have a better life. She needed to have someone who really cared for her and was willing to take care of her. Funny thing is she thought I was the one. I could barely take care of myself. How was I going to take care of a wife? No need to worry about that now.

I felt a hand on my shoulder. It was Tom. I turned and hugged him.

"Let's sit down," he said.

We went to one of the sofas off to the side.

"I know this is a stupid question," he said, "but how are you?"

I shrugged.

"It's the standard question at times like this," he said. "Now you have to give the standard answer."

I looked at him.

"What would that be?"

"Oh, something like 'it's rough, but I'll be okay' or 'I don't know what I'm going to do without her', you know something along those lines."

I tried to smile but couldn't. I don't know if I would ever smile again.

"Thanks," I said.

"Don't mention it. Oh, another standard line. 'We'll get through this'."

"She deserved better, Tom. She didn't deserve to die like she did. She needed to live to a ripe old age and die of natural causes after a happy life."

"Well, my friend, that's something we all wish for, but fate or God or whatever, plays us a different hand. Look at all the other people you know who we say died before their time. I think, sometimes, it's just to see how we'll react."

"Very philosophical," I said.

"Yeah, you get that way running a bar."

People were filing in. Some came to give me their condolences. I didn't know a lot of them. Sheila must have led a life I wasn't aware of. I didn't think I knew this many people much less having this many friends.

Tom left me to tend to business which was allowing the mourners to dote over me. I didn't particularly care for it, but I had to play the game. I just wanted it to be over.

Ollie came in looking sharp as ever. He handed me an envelope.

"We picked something up at the station," he said, "to help with expenses."

I could only look at it.

"Hey, even Ursula chipped in," he smiled.

"Thanks," I said and hugged him.

"How are things going with Ramby?" I asked.

He waved his hand.

"Don't worry about him. You need to concentrate on the business at hand."

We sat down.

"I wanted to kill him when you brought him out. I guess I'll be in Dutch for what I did."

He patted my knee.

"I doubt it," he said. "There are some powers higher than Jack and Ursula."

I looked at him.

"Who?"

He shrugged and I left it alone.

"Making any headway on finding out if he killed Barnett?" I finally asked him.

"Ursula should get a conviction because the slug pulled from Barnett's office matched his rifle and his is the only prints on the rifle."

A lady Ollie knew came up to offer sympathy and a prayer. I thanked her and she went to the casket. She bowed her head and touched Sheila's forehead then left.

Two men in dark suits came in and looked around. Both were tall and wide. One spoke with the director who pointed at me. We stood when they came over.

"Mr. Cameron?" one asked.

"That's me."

He put out his hand.

"Estes Verret with the Barnett Company. This is my associate, Feldon Young."

I introduced Ollie and we shook hands all around.

"I'd like to thank you for what you did."

"What exactly did I do?"

"You caught the man who killed Edwin Barnett."

"Whoa," I said, "Detective Fletcher here did that. I was just helping."

The man turned to Ollie and put out his hand.

"Thank you, detective."

"Part of my job," Ollie said, "but we haven't got a conviction yet. I don't like to get that far ahead."

Young looked around the crowding room.

"Could we go somewhere and talk?"

"Is this something that can wait?" Ollie asked. "Mr. Cameron is going through a rough time."

"Oh, yes, I see," Verret said.

"No," I said, "let's talk. I need to do something other than sit and think."

We moved to a corner of the room reminiscent of the Barnett funeral.

"Mrs. Yvonne Barnett," Verret said, "would like to offer you her thanks for what you've done. You put your life in danger and unfortunately, your friend lost her life. She has two offers for you."

He looked at Ollie.

"I know this is a bad time, but Mrs. Barnett is a woman who likes to get things done quickly."

I held up my hand.

"Which one of you will take Edwin's job at the top?"

They looked at each other.

"That is Mrs. Barnett's decision. It could be someone other than one of us."

"Okay" I said, "back to her offers."

Feldon Young spoke up this time.

"Mrs. Barnett has offered to pay for your friend's funeral."

"Her name is Sheila."

"Yes, she wants to ease your burden for Sheila's funeral expenses if you're willing."

"I'll think about it. Number two."

"She wants you to come to work for the company."

"Doing what?"

"In a security capacity."

I looked at Ollie. He shrugged.

"I'll have to think about that, too."

I could see I wasn't giving them the answers they were looking for.

"What would Mrs. Barnett say if I said no to both offers?"

They didn't look too happy.

"I'll tell you what," I said. "You tell Mrs. Barnett I'll give her my answers personally."

"Yes," Verret said. "I'll guess that will have to do."

I put out my hand to both.

"Thank you for coming by," I said.

We watched them leave.

"Looks like Momma Barnett is not wasting any time," Ollie said.

"You think she'll pull enough strings to get her hands on that journal?"

"I would say so. Money can shut things down or open things up depending on what the donor wants."

I looked at my watch.

"Almost time," I said.

We went back to the sofa.

Maurice Portier Baltimore, IV walked up to the small podium.

"I would like to thank all of you for coming to pay your respects for Miss Sheila Arceneaux. Mr. Lee Cameron would like to say a few words."

I couldn't get off the sofa. My legs wouldn't allow it. Ollie stood and helped me. I wobbled to the podium. I had gone over in my mind what I would say about Sheila, but now it escaped me.

"Thank you," I said after composing myself. "Sheila would be happy to see all her friends here to see her off."

I looked at the casket waiting for her to say something, sit up, do anything to make me realize this was all a dream…or nightmare.

"She was special to me. She served as my secretary and unknown to most she was my best friend and, I guess you could call her my girlfriend. Those that know me knows she deserved better, but she stuck by me. She told me she wanted to get in on the action of being a private detective. I told her it would be dangerous, but she insisted. Then one day we received a threatening letter. She didn't like the sound of it and decided it wasn't for her. Unfortunately, it was too late."

I looked at Ollie. He made a breaking motion. I was rambling. I didn't want to let her go and felt that talking about her would delay the inevitable.

"I would like to echo Mr. Baltimore's words by thanking all of you for being here. Sheila would appreciate it."

Another small service was held at the cemetery. Umbrellas were everywhere. I could hear the rain tapping on the canopy top. I sat between Tom and Ollie in the row of chairs.

I sat for a while when it ended. Tom and Ollie left me to pay my last respects. I went to the casket and put my hand on it.

"I love you, Sheila," I whispered then took my flower out of my lapel and put it on the casket with the rest.

It was time to go, to get on with my life.

My two friends were waiting for me at the car and they had company

Isaac Kruger and Yvonne Barnett.

"Mr. Cameron," she said, "we are sorry for your loss."

"Thanks," I said shaking her hand.

Kruger put out his hand.

"Sorry," was all he said.

I nodded.

"Your two boys came by the funeral home," I said.

"Yes," she said averting her eyes. "I guess that wasn't very thoughtful of me. They were just doing their jobs."

"What did you have in mind?"

She looked at Ollie and Tom.

"You can talk in front of them."

"Okay," she said resuming command. "First, I would like to pay for Sheila Arceneaux's funeral. I feel it's the least I can do."

"Why?"

"My daughter-in-law got you into this. It's my contribution."

"Neda didn't get me into anything. I got myself into it."

"I see."

"I'll make this easy for you, Mrs. Barnett," I said. "I will pay for Sheila's funeral. It is not your responsibility, but I appreciate the thought. I hope you understand I have to do it myself."

"Yes, I can understand that."

"Now," I said, "on the job offer. I like doing what I do. I would be happy to do work for you or your company in the future, but I prefer to be my own boss."

"I'll keep that in mind."

She started to say something else but changed her mind.

"I guess we'll go now."

Isaac Kruger shook all our hands but didn't say anything. They went to a large car Kruger was driving.

"Oh, Mrs. Barnett," I said. "I'm sure the parish would like some help with Philo Griggs."

She nodded and smiled.

"I'm sure they would."

I found out later that she went back to the funeral home and paid for both funerals. I sent her a thank you card and a stern message to mind her own business.

Crystal came running up as they drove off.

"I'm sorry, Lee, I couldn't make it," she said out of breath.

"Don't worry about it. I'm sure you had things you had to do."

"Part of the job."

It was at this time Ollie and Tom decided it was time to go. I hugged them both and thanked them for being there.

"You have a special relationship with them," she said.

"They're good friends."

"You think I'll ever make your good friends list?"

I shrugged.

"Sheila and I talked about our situation."

I nodded.

"We were getting back to being friends again."

"That's good."

"Look, Lee, I don't know what to say."

"It's hard, isn't it? You have this job where all you do is say things, or in your case print things then something like this happens and you draw a blank. It's humbling."

"You've changed, haven't you?"

We walked to her car.

"I don't know it yet. Death changes the survivors in ways they may not be aware of, but it's too early to tell with me."

"Look, if you need something, let me know. Maybe we can work together in the future."

"You didn't have much luck on this one."

She smiled and opened the door of her car.

"More than you think."

"I don't want to know."

"Why don't we get together sometime?" she asked.

"Off the record?"

"Off the record."

"I'll think about it."

"Let me know."

I watched her drive off and took one last look at the casket. They were waiting for everyone to leave so they could finish their job. I guess it is easier when everyone is gone, and the family can't see the last thing to be done after death.

17

Since you, the reader, stuck with me this long I owe you a conclusion to the story. It's been a few months now since Sheila's funeral and Ollie's arrest of Hastings Ramby.

I'm looking to move out of my office at the bank building. I don't want to be there without Sheila. I decided I could cope better being in a new environment.

Neda Barnett received her life insurance for Edwin Barnett's death. She is not involved in any way with the company. As far as I know she never was. She still takes her monthly trips, but they are not covered like they use to be. She has the money, but not the attention. I thought it strange she didn't move away from the area. She is the only who knows why that is. She pops up at various charity functions and galas. She is big into Mardi Gras in the area.

Yvonne Barnett reorganized the company then sold it and moved to some Caribbean Island. She said she was getting up in age and wanted to enjoy what was left of her life. There are no blood relatives to spend time with. I heard through the grapevine she'll leave her entire estate to her favorite charities which will remain anonymous until the time of her death. She calls me on occasion and tells me she will keep me in mind if she needs any detective work. I'm not holding my breath on that one.

Oliver "Ollie" Fletcher remains with the Shelberg Police Force as the top ranked detective. He is one of my best friends and I am glad for him. We still get together.

Doreen Tilly stayed with the new company as secretary to the new chairman. After Sheila's funeral she called me to offer her condolences. She cried so much she could barely talk so the conversation was short. She did tell me she wished she would have let us know about the journal sooner. It may have helped, or it may not. We'll never know.

Crystal Hudson is still the fireball reporter for the *Shelberg Beacon*. We see each other now and then socially. I follow her stories, but it's hard not to since she tends to get the big ones. Rumor has it she'll receive some kind of newspaper award later in the year. I wish her luck. We still talk about the Edwin Barnett murder case. She wants to know if there was something we missed that may have prevented Hastings Ramby from killing Sheila and Philo Griggs. I wish her luck with that, too. We never did have to use bogus information to flush out Ramby. He did that on his own. I often wonder how long it would have taken us if he would have lain low.

Isaac Kruger pulled the strangest stunt of all. He resigned from the law firm he started and built up to one of the most respected, if not feared, group of attorneys in the state. He is now Yvonne Barnett's personal lawyer. He travels with her. When she returns to the states for whatever endeavor she has in mind, Isaac is at her side. Is there something naughty going on? That's what everyone wants to know, especially the tabloids. What juicy gossip that would make. If there is anything going between them, it is kept secret. So far no one has been able to dig up any mud on them. If someone does, I wouldn't be surprised if it is Crystal.

Jack Vincent retired from the police force following Hastings Ramby's arrest. He said it was time for him to get out. He'd let the younger people handle the case. The last I heard he moved to Southern Florida and runs a fishing charter. The guys at the station get cards from him. Ollie told me he looks good. I guess we mended our fences, but I don't really know. I doubt if he cares. I hope he does well with his new business.

Melody Broussard isn't planning to run for re-election as Shelberg Mayor. She is in the early stages of putting together some unknown enterprise; unknown to us anyway.

Ursula Daniels is chomping at the bit to get Hastings Ramby into the courtroom. She feels this could be her big chance to jump from district attorney to state attorney general. She is still one of the most aggressive district attorneys in the state. If Ramby is indicted, she'll use whatever is at her disposal to convict him. She will go after the death penalty. We speak on occasion, but our conversations are short and to the point. I don't think she likes me.

Xavier Unger dropped by one day to tell me thanks for what I tried to do for Philo. He felt it gave Philo some credibility in an otherwise fruitless life. He said it was sad Philo had to die the way he did, but he died trying to save the life of another. He said Philo was happy when I talked to him about guarding Sheila. It showed I trusted him. I was one of the few who would, Xavier said. He goes to the cemetery to keep Philo's grave neat. He said it was the least he could do, but he wouldn't do it for just anyone of his clients, if that's what they are called.

I see Ira Quint's picture in the paper all the time. It seems the guy is as good a bowler as he claims. He called one day to say he was trying for the pro tour and quitting the Port. He was chasing after his dream. Only time will tell. He's arrogant and confident. That might help him. I believe he's a bit old to go against more experienced younger guys, but what does he have to lose? I wish him luck.

Uriah Klug is plugging along as Greenwood Parish Coroner. He is easily identified with his spiked hair. Some of the higher ups would like him to retire, but he keeps getting re-elected. The voters are obviously satisfied with this work.

Tom Jones is my other best friend. I visit The Tenth Inning on a regular basis. We talk about everything except the Edwin Barnett mess. It's awkward, but we avoid it. I'm sure, or hope, it will improve as time moves on. I'm glad I have him and Ollie to lean on.

Feldon Young and Estes Verret disappeared from view. I looked for their names when Yvonne Barnett sold the company but didn't see them anywhere. I guess the new owner didn't want them around.

Lavender Giles, Naomi Queen, Peggy Rogers and Selma Wicks were the four women we saw at the cemetery for Edwin Barnett's funeral. I'm sure you figured it out along the way. Tom tells me they visit regularly and sit away from the other customers. No one knows what they talk about. I could guess. Crystal told me she tried to get them to talk about Barnett, but they refused to say anything concerning their benefactor or his death.

Mabel Ramby filed for divorce from Hastings. She called to tell me she appreciated what we did for her although I don't know what that could be. We didn't treat her like a criminal. That could be it. She told me she was moving to another town. Shelberg has too many bad memories for her to stay. She also didn't want to be identified as the wife of the man who killed the richest man in the state although that hasn't been the case, not yet.

Hastings Ramby is still in jail. He's being held without bail. The investigation is ongoing, but Ollie feels they will soon have enough evidence to indict him. I think he waited for me to pump him about what he had. That's what I would have done in the past, but not now. I'm not interested. Chances are he'll be tried for the murder of Philo Griggs. That looks to be the obvious one. Crystal is their star witness. If he gets the death penalty, I'll be there. I regret not finishing what I started that day in the parking lot the day he was arrested. Maybe I'll get over it. Maybe I won't. I did hear that Mabel talked to him not to long after his arrest. She wanted him to confess, but he wouldn't. She left him soon after.

I'm sitting in my small apartment putting all this down. My nights are restless, but they are getting better. It doesn't take me near as long to fall asleep. I never in my wildest imagination dreamed this is what it would be like at this time in my life. I feel an empty void inside, but I have to say Tom, Ollie, and even Crystal tries to drag me out of my doldrums. I need to get on another case to occupy me...and it would help with the bills.

Even at my advanced age of 35, Sheila was my first love. I had crushes in school and even some along the way, but she was the first woman I truly loved. That may sound strange for some, but my love life has never been the greatest or even good.

Like I said at the beginning, I'm moving out of my office. I'm looking for something small. I won't need a secretary. This time around, I'll handle everything myself. My business is not really big enough for a full-time secretary. And I will continue to work alone. I like the freedom.

I go to the cemetery to see Sheila. I wipe off her headstone like I would wipe a tear from her cheek. I sit and talk just like she could hear. She might hear everything I say for all I know. If so, I hope she approves. They keep the cemetery neat and clean, but I bring a brush anyway and clean it myself if I think it needs it. Sometimes I do it just to do it. It may be therapy for me. I don't know what a shrink would say.

Philo is buried in the same cemetery in a section reserved for those not claimed by family. It's sad, but what can one do? I never had the chance to thank him for trying to save Sheila. I hope by trusting him, he would think that would be my thanks.

I try to go often and see both of them.

As time goes by, my tears are fewer and the battles with my emotions are not as bad. I hope it's because of time and not my lack of caring for either. Time doesn't heal the wounds. It makes the wounds easier to bear. I know I'll get past this because I have to or go crazy. I don't want to spend the rest of my life in a rubber room screaming her name and banging my head on the wall even if said wall is padded. I want to adjust because that is the sanest thing to do. I want to be able to talk about it with other people without losing control of my mind. I want to be able to remember enough some nights to cry myself to sleep.

I hope my little monologue here ties up the loose ends. I realize I don't have anything new to say about Hastings Ramby, but it could go on for years. The best I can hope for at this time is he'll get his for Philo Griggs. Philo deserves that much.

It's time I finish this up. I have to meet Ollie and Crystal at Tom's place. Until we cross paths again, remember one thing.

If you have good friends, lean on them when you're having a bad day. Let them lean on you when they are having a bad day.

It helped and is still helping me.

One more thing. Sheila never did take those karate lessons.

www.ingramcontent.com/pod-product-compliance
Lightning Source LLC
Chambersburg PA
CBHW072221150726

48002CB00005B/1917